Franco's Fortune

By

Cara Marsi

Franco's Fortune
Cara Marsi

Copyright © 2013 Carolyn Matkowsky
Published by The Painted Lady Press
United States of America

Print ISBN: 978-0-9915975-4-3
Kindle ASIN: B00BNA3JQI

Discover other titles by Cara Marsi at CaraMarsi.com
Edited by Laura Kelly
Formatted by Aileen Fish
Cover by Harris Channing

"When a female bodyguard is hired to protect a rich playboy, she finds saving his life is easier than protecting her heart."

When the past and present collide...

Somebody wants rich playboy Franco Callahan dead. When security expert Josephine Fortune arrives on his doorstep thanks to his sister Doriana, Franco finds it hard to refuse. He's had a secret attraction for the diminutive bodyguard since they met at Doriana's wedding five years before.

But attraction is all it is. Combat boot-clad Jo is *not* the kind of woman Franco usually loves and leaves. Which makes the ruse that Jo is his new live-in girlfriend just that until Jo gets a makeover. Suddenly seduction is on his mind and Franco has all the time in the world to pursue it—and Jo.

Martial artist Jo can take down men twice her size without blinking, but Franco's appeal outmaneuvers her emotional defenses. Jo's tough exterior hides a dark past, and Franco seems determined to learn her every secret. But he has secrets of his own.

The more Franco gets to know Jo, the more he realizes he needs her in his life, and not as his bodyguard. But as the threats to Franco escalate, Jo must use every one of her combat skills to protect him.

Can Jo keep both Franco and her heart safe, or will they pay the ultimate price for love?

CHAPTER ONE

Franco Callahan slammed the door to his Delancey Street townhouse and hurried into the April morning, glancing at his watch as he ran down the steps. He was late. He'd wanted to get to work early. He had a busy day ahead. His mind on the Connecticut casino bid and the pile of work waiting on his desk, he strode along the uneven pavement to his black Mercedes parked at the other end of the narrow street.

He answered his ringing phone as he hurried toward his car, and heard a deep male voice rasp, "You didn't get our message the first time, Callahan. You've forced us to play dirty. Give us the money and we might let you live."

The menace in the stranger's voice chilled Franco, tightening his gut. "Who is this?"

"Maybe you'll listen to our new message." The call disconnected.

Franco stared down at his phone.

An ear-splitting boom rent the air, vibrating the ground beneath his feet. The blast sent Franco on his rear, the breath knocked out of him. Ears ringing, struggling to sit, he saw a ball of fire at the end of the street. Flames licked at what was left of his car.

4

One Week Later

"Heard you need a bodyguard, Callahan."

The sultry female voice jerked Franco's attention from his computer. He swiveled his chair and glanced toward his office doorway. A thrill shot through him at the sight of the petite redhead, arms folded across her chest, leaning impudently against the doorjamb. He tamped down the excitement she always aroused in him and narrowed his eyes.

"Well, if it isn't Josephine Fortune. What are you doing here?"

She stepped into the room and deposited her duffel bag on the floor. "I'm real glad to see you too, Callahan. And the name is Jo."

The tough little spitfire rarely wore anything other than camouflage fatigues, T-shirts, and combat boots. He couldn't help noticing the way her khaki-colored T-shirt stretched over her firm breasts and the way her full, pink lips—kissable lips—parted. She wasn't his type he reminded himself, not for the first time in their five-year association. His type was tall, blonde, leggy, and a tigress in bed—not a fireball more comfortable on the shooting range than between satin sheets. He shot her an insolent smile, retreating into the playboy persona he showed the world.

Her green eyes, translucent and light as a spring leaf, studied him. "Logan and Doriana sent me to protect your sorry ass."

His eyes never leaving hers, he stood. "I told them I don't need protection. I'm sorry you had to come all this way. Go back to Tucson."

Tension in every line of her toned body, she moved closer. "I don't like this any more than you do, Callahan.

Think I want to spend my time babysitting some spoiled playboy? As far as I'm concerned, if one of your bimbos has it in for you, that's your problem."

"Then leave."

"No can do. Logan's my boss. He sent me to keep someone from killing you and that's what I'm going to do."

The fear that was his constant companion these days pressed against his chest. Masking his feeling of vulnerability, he flattened his palms on his desk. "Tell Logan and Doriana thanks, but the Philadelphia police are handling the case. I don't need a bodyguard."

She moved even closer and leaned over the desk until their faces were inches apart. The woman had guts. He had to hand that to her. He wondered if anything scared her. A familiar scent surrounded her, teasing his nostrils. Grapefruit? On her the fruity aroma smelled tantalizing and seductive. Jo Fortune, seductive? He moved back from temptation.

She straightened and stepped away from his desk. "Sure, I'd rather be in sunny Arizona than rainy Philadelphia. But Doriana's not too keen on her brother getting killed. So you're stuck with me until the cops get whoever's after you."

He studied her and something stirred in him, the same feeling he'd had minutes ago; the feeling he'd gotten the first time he'd met her at Logan and Doriana's wedding five years before, and every time after that. As an honorary member of the Callahan-Tanner clan, Jo was present at family holidays and functions. For all her smart mouth and bluster, he recognized the hurt that shadowed her eyes and softened her generous mouth. A part of him wanted to find out who put that hurt there and to take it away if he could. Jo brought out a protectiveness in him that scared him nearly as much as the thought of someone killing him.

Franco sank into his chair and gestured to the chair facing his desk. "Sit, Josephine, and we'll talk."

She sat and crossed her booted feet at the ankles. "It's Jo, Callahan."

He suppressed a smile. "And it's Franco, Fortune."

A glimmer of amusement shone in her eyes. "All right. A truce. You call me Jo and I'll call you Franco."

"Agreed, since you've come all this way." He settled back in his chair. "Why did Logan send you without telling me?"

She held out her palms. "Logan figured once I showed up, you wouldn't send me away."

"He figured wrong. How did you get past my security?"

"Your father contacted the head of building security. They were expecting me. I only had to show my ID." Her lips quirked in a faint smile. "It helped that your assistant is at lunch too. We timed it just right."

"My father knows?" The old, familiar insecurity knotted his gut. "I run this company."

"He still owns it."

And he still owns you. The unspoken words were clear in her tone.

With effort, he dislodged the unsettling thought. Four years ago he'd been forced to turn his life around when his dad had a stroke. Then there was the situation with Mac, the betrayal that had Franco questioning all he stood for, all he'd worked for. A double whammy that had shifted his world on its axis. After a rough start, he'd done a good job with the company, bringing in more revenue every year, expanding into even more countries. Yet, the force that was Dan Callahan was imprinted on Callahan Construction.

Franco positioned himself more comfortably and concentrated on his immediate problem—the slim redhead sitting before him. He gave her his smoothest smile, one that had won over beautiful women and business sharks alike. "I appreciate Logan sending you, but I told him I'll be okay. I have faith in the police," he lied expertly.

Jo gripped the arms of her chair and leaned forward. "The police haven't done beans so far. Someone breaks into your house two weeks ago and rips it apart. Then your car is blown up. And they don't even have a suspect."

Franco loosened his tie, feeling suddenly warm. He'd tried to push the incidents out of his mind, but they were always there, threatening his peace, his control. His life.

He scanned her again. She was pretty, with those eyes, those sharp cheekbones and those kissable lips. He cleared his throat. "No offense, Jo, but what can you do for me? You're what? Five foot one, a hundred pounds? I'm five eleven and I work out. I'd beat you in any kind of a fight any day. How can you possibly act as my bodyguard?"

Sitting straighter, she grinned. "You think you can beat me, Callahan? Care to find out?"

He laughed. "Simmer down. I don't fight women, no matter who they are."

She sobered. "Look, Callahan—uh, Franco, I'm good at what I do. No one is going to hurt you while I'm around. And my size makes it easy to fool people. I'll protect you."

He loosened his tie some more. "And you expect to be with me 24/7? I don't see that happening. What about when you're not with me? Whoever is after me could strike then. It won't work. Tell that to Logan."

"I'm not going anywhere. We'll make it work. I'll

move in with you. That's Logan's plan."

"What? Us, living together? I don't think so." He moved out from behind the desk and began to pace. "And what will I tell people? I have a pint-sized bodyguard because I'm afraid? No, absolutely not."

She moved too, cutting off his route and facing him. "Logan and Doriana care about you and they want you safe. I'll keep you safe."

The sparks flying from her eyes hit Franco like shards of glass. He couldn't admit to anyone—least of all, her—that the thought of someone trying to kill him scared the crap out of him. After the two incidents, a thought had niggled at his brain. Was someone from his party-guy past out to get revenge, or worse? He'd done some things he was ashamed of. Were they coming back to bite him? He didn't want to put Jo in danger, yet he had no choice. He was outflanked.

"Earth to Franco."

Jo's voice dumped him back to the present. He leveled his gaze at her. "I wouldn't want anyone to know I've got a bodyguard. So what story do we tell to explain us living together?"

She gave him a self-satisfied smirk. "So you've agreed to let me help you?"

He shook his head. "I haven't agreed to anything. I'm curious to know what story you and Logan concocted."

She lifted one T-shirt clad shoulder. "Simple. We tell people I'm your girlfriend."

◇◇◇

Shock registered on his face. If she weren't so pissed off over this whole assignment, Jo would have enjoyed Franco's reaction. She expected him to start sputtering any minute. She didn't want to be here any more than he wanted her here. But Logan had sent her, and she owed Logan her life. She'd do anything for him and Doriana.

"No way," he said. "No one will believe you're my girlfriend. You're not my type."

Hurt came out of nowhere and kicked her in the stomach. Almost against her will, her gaze swept him. God, he was beautiful, with his GQ-model high cheekbones, those chiseled lips, and those wide shoulders under the beautifully cut suit, a suit that probably cost more than her whole wardrobe. Of course, no one would expect the rich, powerful, gorgeous Franco Callahan of having a girlfriend who looked like her. She swallowed, mustering her pride.

She hated that she'd always been attracted to the spoiled playboy. Yet, looking at him now, she saw the subtle changes in him—the strands of gray in his short dark hair, the seriousness in the depth of his light blue Irish eyes, eyes that gave no hint of the Italian heritage that flowed through him also. Fine lines of tension bracketed his mouth. Had running an international company done that to him? Gone was the arrogant player she'd first met years ago, the one who swaggered through life, a blonde babe on his arm. He'd changed and she'd been too busy fighting her attraction to him to notice.

He must have ticked off someone bad enough to want him dead. Years in the security business had her mind whirling with possible scenarios. Maybe one of his old girlfriends was out for some sort of revenge. Except the women she'd met didn't seem to have the smarts to come up with a vendetta.

"Jo, I'm not doing this. I'll take my chances."

His words pulled her from her jumbled thoughts. She sucked in a breath and looked at him. "It's not your choice.

I'm staying."

His eyes narrowed and he shot her a wicked grin. It made him look somehow sexier and sent unwanted pleasure rocketing through her. He walked around her, scrutinizing her. Then he stood in front of her again, so close she could smell his cologne, no doubt expensive, with just a hint of sandalwood. Everything about him reeked of money. He was so out of her league. She shook her head as if she could dislodge her disquieting thoughts. He was a job. Nothing more.

He touched her chin with his fingers and tilted her face until their eyes met. "Maybe you'll do."

She jerked free. "What are you up to?"

"My cousin Anita is the best stylist in the city. She can do something with that hair." He touched her braid where it rested on her shoulder. His eyes darkened, and he brushed a finger over her lips. Her skin tingled where he touched. She should pull away, but she didn't want to. She'd spent untold nights lying in her bed, her lonely bed, thinking of him. The thought hit her like a splash of icy Delaware River water.

She stepped back, putting distance between them. She didn't need a man, especially a rich guy who'd had the world handed to him. Besides, no decent man would want her. Hadn't she been told that before?

A mischievous gleam glinted in Franco's eyes. "If you're so hell bent on masquerading as my girlfriend, you have to look the part. We'll get you a new hairdo, new wardrobe, make you into the kind of woman I'd take as my lover."

"No. Take me as I am. Don't think you can chase me away by threatening to turn me into a sexpot. You need me."

He waved a hand. "You want this charade, you play by my rules."

"What will your real girlfriend say if she sees me all

glammed up? It'll be easier to convince her to go along with this if I'm myself." The thought of Franco and any lover tugged at her heart, swirling sadness through her. She'd seen him numerous times, always parading a leggy blonde. It shouldn't bother her now. Yet, it did.

"I haven't had a girlfriend in more than six months."

"Losing your touch, Callahan?"

He moved closer. "Not a chance, sweetheart."

She glared at him, then released a resigned sigh. "I'll go along with your rules."

He gave her another of his wicked smiles that made excitement jolt all the way to her toes.

"Game on," he said.

CHAPTER TWO

Franco was sure he'd seen hurt in her beautiful green eyes when he'd voiced what they both knew—Jo Fortune wasn't his type. Even though he'd known her for years, there were depths to her he couldn't fathom.

She'd lifted her chin, defiance in her stance. Truth be told, he enjoyed sparring with her. Jo was a lot more fascinating than most of the women he'd dated. She took as good as she gave, and she never gave an inch. Yet, there was something different about her now, a new softness that brought her vulnerability closer to the surface. He hadn't meant to hurt her.

"I have a ton of work, as you can see." He waved a hand over his desk. "I'll be here until late. I don't have time now to discuss all the ramifications of this…this situation. But I do have some questions that can't wait. Sit." He gestured for her to sit again.

She arched an eyebrow but sat down, crossing one booted foot over her ankle. "What questions? Shoot."

He sat too, then leaned forward, locking his gaze with hers. "I get why you and my brother-in-law have concocted this whole scenario. But it's not a good idea. People who know me won't buy it. I've never lived with a woman."

"Really?"

"I like my space." *And I've never found any woman in-*

teresting enough to have around 24/7. Franco had the feeling that living with Jo Fortune would be very interesting.

Jo rolled her eyes. "I'll bet you love your space."

He ignored her jibe. "Even if we could convince people you're my live-in girlfriend, you can't be with me every minute. I have a company to run, and you can't come with me to work every day."

She uncrossed her legs and grinned. "Logan is smarter than that. He knew you'd need two bodyguards. That's why he hired Harris."

Franco rubbed a hand down his face. "Why don't you and Logan just take over my life?"

"Settle down." She gave a small laugh. "Logan isn't about to let a family member be killed, spoiled playboy or not."

He blew out a breath and let the playboy remark pass. He'd probably never live down his reputation. Did he care? Yeah, on some level he did. "Who is Harris?"

"He's a PI slash bodyguard, an ex-SEAL our firm uses when we need someone investigated or if some hotshot CEO on the East Coast needs protection. As you well know, considering that Logan caught the perp trying to bring down this company five years ago, our security firm specializes in corporate espionage and protection. What Logan did for Callahan Construction got our firm lots of high profile cases. Harris has guarded some major CEO's. So have I. You'd be surprised what kinds of trouble those guys can get themselves into." She folded her arms across her chest. "We haven't lost one yet."

A soft female voice diverted Franco's attention to the doorway. "Franco. Excuse me." His assistant, Ruth, stood there, a frown on her face.

"What is it, Ruth?"

She looked at Jo then back at him. "I'm sorry I wasn't here earlier. You didn't tell me you had an appointment."

"Jo's a friend," he lied. Might as well start the charade now, in case he decided to go along with this crazy scheme. "What's up?"

"There's someone else here to see you. He says his name is Harris. He doesn't have an appointment either."

"It's okay, Ruth. Show him in." These people really were determined to take over his life.

A barrel-chested middle-aged guy, gray-haired and dressed in a well-cut black suit, sauntered into the office. Jo stood and nodded to the guy. "Harris. It's good to see you again, man."

Harris gave an imperceptible nod toward Jo. "You're lookin' good, darlin'. But then you always look good."

An arrow of jealousy hit Franco like a shot between the eyes. He definitely wasn't thinking straight.

Hand held out, the guy headed toward him. "Hello, Mr. Callahan, I'm Harris. I assume Jo's been fillin' you in."

"A little." Franco came around his desk and shook the man's hand. "Harris what?"

The other guy grinned. "Just Harris."

"Call me Franco." He looked over to find his assistant hovering in the doorway. "Everything's fine, Ruth. You can leave us. Would you shut the door please?"

Still frowning, Ruth softly closed the door.

"Please sit, Harris." Franco gestured to a second chair facing his desk. The burly Harris lowered himself into the chair. Jo sat down as well. Franco eased into his chair and shifted his gaze between the two of them. Was something going on between them? He dismissed the thought, and tamped down another hit of ridiculous jealousy. The guy was old enough to be her father and didn't seem like Jo's type, whatever that was.

"Franco doesn't like the idea of my pretending to be his girlfriend and living with him," Jo said with a glance at Harris. "He says I'm not his type."

"Why not?" Harris shifted in his seat. "Any man would want this lady on his arm." Grinning, he edged forward, his brown eyes on Franco. "I could move in with you if you don't want Jo."

Franco brushed a hand over his hair. He didn't see any way out of this mess. If he wanted to stay alive, he'd have to go along with their plan. But a choice between Harris and Jo? A no-brainer.

He grabbed a pen from his desk and squeezed his fingers around it, pressing away his annoyance. "I don't like this whole situation. I like my privacy, but I am in a jam. Privacy isn't worth much if I'm not alive to enjoy it. So, it looks like I have to go along with you. No offense, Harris, but I don't think anyone will believe you're my girlfriend." He dropped his pen and gave Jo what he hoped was a pointed look. "Jo can play the part, but I'm not so sure anyone's going to believe that either."

"We've already been through that, Callahan," she muttered.

Did he imagine the twinge of hurt in her voice? A spasm of regret tugged at him. "Remember what we agreed."

Her clear green eyes, shadowed now, met his. "I said I'd do it. Sheesh. You don't believe me?"

He gave her his most flirtatious grin, trying to put the sparkle back in her eyes. "No, not entirely."

"What am I missing?" Harris asked.

"Franco wants to glam me up so people are more likely to believe I'm his latest girlfriend."

"You, glammed up?" Harris laughed. "That I've got to see."

Her faced pinked.

Franco had never known her to be so sensitive. He missed his sparring partner, yet this new side of Jo made him want to take her into his arms and comfort her. That was a thought he needed to diffuse.

Jo straightened and looked at him with a sober expression, all business now. "We'd better get started, map out our plans. And we have questions for you."

He nodded. "Go ahead."

"I need my tablet." Jo strode to her duffel bag and knelt to open it. She slipped a tablet out and powered it up as she walked back to the desk.

As she settled into her chair, Harris dug into his jacket pocket and pulled out a few pieces of wrapped hard candy. He held them out to Jo and Franco, who both declined. Harris unwrapped a piece and popped it into his mouth.

"Since I gave up smoking a few years ago, I'm never without this candy," Harris said.

Jo grinned at Harris. "Candy is better than cigarettes, my friend."

Fingers poised over her tablet, she turned to Franco. "What's happened since your car was blown up? Any more phone calls?"

"A couple," he said. "The guy always threatens to kill me if I don't give him the money."

Harris bit down on his candy. "What money?"

Franco let out a frustrated sigh. "I have no idea. Believe me, if I knew, I'd give him the money to save my life."

"Is it always the same person who calls?" Jo asked

"I think so."

Jo typed in some notes, then looked at him. "What are the police doing?"

"They can't trace the calls. They've set up extra patrols in my neighborhood, but the police are short-staffed and can't give me a lot of protection."

"More reason you need us," Jo said. "Anything else?"

"I've already told the police, but here goes. I came out of my house last Saturday morning to go for a run and a black Escalade drove by. Someone fired shots from the car."

"What?" Jo's head came up. "They blow up your car, then fire shots in your direction?"

He waved away her concern, if that was indeed what it was. "They didn't hit anywhere near me. I figured it was another threat. If they'd wanted to kill me, they would have."

"No more going anywhere alone and no more morning runs until this is over," she said. "Tell us everything, and don't leave out anything."

Jo flopped on the beige silk comforter in Franco's spacious guest room and put her hands behind her head, staring at the ceiling, painted white in stark contrast to the dark green walls. Harris had driven her in his bullet-proof Town Car to Franco's Delancey Street townhouse fifteen minutes ago, then left to return to Callahan Construction, where he'd settle in to keep Franco safe while he was at work. She smiled, thinking how uncomfortable Franco was over this whole situation.

He wasn't used to anyone giving him orders, that was for sure. But if he wanted to save his life, he'd learn to listen to Harris and her. They made a good team.

Despite the work Franco kept insisting he needed to get back to, she and Harris had grilled him for forty-five minutes, getting the names of his friends, acquaintances, business associates, past and present, and former girlfriends. No one was above suspicion. He'd squirmed a little when they'd asked about his women. Surprising that he didn't have a woman in his life now.

For the first time since she'd known him, Franco Callahan was available. She tamped down the pleasure that began to build in her. But she couldn't stop herself from wondering what it would be like to kiss him. Then her mind veered to imagine the feel of those full lips on her mouth, trailing down her body. Fear slammed into her, shattering the fantasy. She couldn't go there. She knew where it led—knew the hurt and the guilt.

She slid from the bed before her mind could betray her again with dreams of what could never be. She'd been sent here to do a job. Forcing her thoughts back to their elaborate plans, she unpacked her duffel bag quickly and put her clothes in the dresser drawers. The one closet in the room was bigger than her bedroom back in Tucson. Now it was empty, but soon it'd be filled with the kinds of clothes Franco insisted she needed. Anxiety twisted in her gut. *Haute couture* wasn't her style. She'd look like a fool. Her face flushed at the thought of Franco laughing at her.

In an effort to keep busy and focus on her job, Jo decided on a quick tour of the large townhouse, decorated with modern furnishings. Entering the room next to hers, she saw it was a media room, outfitted with the latest TV and sound system and comfortable-looking chairs, perfect for TV or movie viewing or listening to music.

Two framed photographs on a side table snagged her

attention, pulling her from visions of soft music and Franco. She strode toward the table and lifted one of the photos. Franco's parents, Lena and Dan, smiled from the picture. Dressed casually in slacks and silk shirt, petite, dark-haired Lena looked the epitome of the stylish matron. Dan, an older, slightly shorter version of Franco, and dressed in slacks and a golf shirt, had his arm around his wife. A sophisticated, handsome couple, good parents who loved their children and grandchildren. Jo's mouth tilted in a wry smile. She sure didn't know anything about parental love. That had died along with her father.

She set down the photo of Dan and Lena and picked up the other one, a picture of Doriana and Logan with their two kids—Josh, almost twenty-one and Lenamarie, three—taken in the backyard of their house in Tucson. Other than his black hair, Josh was the image of Logan, with chiseled features and wide-set shoulders. He must drive the girls at college crazy. Little Lenamarie, named after her grandmother and great-grandmother, had Logan's dark blond hair and Doriana's golden-brown eyes. Joy radiated from the family's big smiles. Jo doubted she'd ever find the kind of contentment Logan and Doriana shared. They were wonderful people and deserved all the happiness in the world.

With a sigh, Jo set the picture back on the table. She strode to the windows, checking them as she had the windows in her room, making sure they were securely locked. From the rough outline Franco had given her of his house, she knew another bedroom plus his suite were on this floor. She'd check them all.

On the ride over, Harris had told her that homes on Delancey Street were some of the highest priced and most historic homes in Old City Philadelphia. He needn't have bothered. The street reeked of money, old money. Delicate trees, just starting to bud, formed a perfect canopy for the stately townhouses with their marble steps and high ceilings. Nothing in Tucson could compare.

She descended the stairs, passing from the small foyer into the large living room. That room and the adjoining dining room were designer showpieces, the walls painted sage green. A cream-colored leather sectional and chairs dominated the living room, with a small teak wood bar tucked into a corner. Bottles of high quality liquor and wine lined mirrored shelves behind the bar. Tied-back ivory drapes over sheer curtains of the same color covered the large multi-paned windows. Museum quality paintings hung on the walls, and fresh flowers in pops of bright colors sat in exquisite Murano-style vases on glass-topped tables around the room. The dining room overlooked the enclosed backyard. A pale wood dining table that looked like it could seat twenty easily was flanked by high-backed chairs upholstered in sage green and cream. She stood between the two rooms and let her gaze roam. A real showplace, like something out of *Architectural Digest*. Dramatic and glamorous, yet somehow comfortable.

A place made for seduction.

Willing those thoughts away once again, she headed into the large kitchen, with its gleaming white walls, high-end stainless appliances and ceiling height cabinets. She tried the back door, making sure the deadbolt held. Someone had broken in through the back door and ransacked the place just two weeks ago. She shook her head at Franco's admission that he hadn't had a security system at the time and had had one installed last week. Damn the man! Living in a house like this with no security system. She'd get someone to replace the back door with a steel one. She checked the basement last. Satisfied all was secure there, she headed back to the kitchen.

As she sat at the granite center counter to type in some notes, a sound permeated the quiet. She froze. There it was again. A key turning in the front door lock, then the door opening and closing. Jo hadn't reset the security alarm. The hairs on her nape stood up.

She glanced at the clock on the microwave. Franco wasn't expected home for hours, and Harris would call when they were on the way. She pulled her Glock from the waistband of her pants. Cautiously she crept out of the kitchen, staying close to the walls, and made her way to the living room. Adrenaline pumping and her body on alert, she primed herself to fight. Hugging the dining room wall, she peered into the living room. A young dark-haired woman holding a huge tote bag stared back at her.

"Who are you?" Jo raised her gun. "You'd better talk if you know what's good for you."

Fear in her eyes, the woman dropped the bag and ran for the door. "Stop!" Jo shouted.

Trembling, the woman turned around, her hands raised.

"Start talking," Jo growled.

CHAPTER THREE

"Please," the woman sobbed. "Mr. Franco give me key. He say all okay. I'm legal."

"Mr. Franco? Legal?" Jo lowered her gun. "It's okay. I'm a friend of Mr. Franco's."

The woman put her arms at her sides and backed away. Terror shone in her deep brown eyes. She blinked rapidly. No more than twenty-five, her long-sleeved T-shirt and ragged jeans hung from her skinny frame. With a shaking hand, she brushed back strands of black hair that had come loose from her ponytail.

Pity for the woman tugged at Jo's heart, but she tensed, ready to defend herself if needed. She'd learned the hard way that the most innocent-looking people could be the most lethal. "I won't hurt you," Jo said. "What are you doing here?"

"I clean for Mr. Franco. See?" The woman pointed to the large tote bag she'd dropped. Her attention riveted on the woman, Jo reached over and picked up the bag, dumping its contents. Cleaning supplies fell onto the Oriental rug.

Relaxing slightly, Jo blew out a breath. "Why did you try to run?"

The woman folded her arms across her chest and backed farther away. "Mr. Franco's lawyer say I okay. Please don't send me back to Mexico. Family here."

The woman was truly frightened or she was one hell

23

of an actress. Jo's instincts told her to believe the woman. They'd asked Franco if anyone had keys and he'd said no. He'd lied.

"No one's sending you anywhere," Jo said. She engaged the safety on her gun and tucked it back into her waistband. "Let's gather up this stuff and you can leave."

"I have to clean."

"Okay, since you're here you can clean. But you can't come back for awhile."

"I no clean, Mr. Franco no pay."

"Don't worry. He'll pay."

Frustration had Jo pacing the living room, unable to keep her churning nerves under control. She'd double checked all the locks again, written her lists. She mentally ticked off the items that needed to be second nature while she was on this assignment. Gun with her at all times: check; security alarm set at all times: check.

She'd probably worn a path in the expensive-looking Oriental carpet by now. She glanced at her watch for the hundredth time. A little past seven. Harris had phoned that he and Franco were on their way. Her stomach rumbled, reminding her she hadn't eaten since the sandwich she'd had several hours ago. Food could wait. Her confrontation with Franco couldn't.

Twenty minutes and more miles of pacing later, she heard a car pull up. Over the rumble of the engine, doors opened and closed. Jo hurried to look out the door's peephole, then disengaged the security alarm. Heavy footsteps raced up the marble steps, then the sound of a key turned in the lock.

"See you tomorrow, Franco," she heard Harris say as

the door swung open.

Franco entered the foyer and shut the door behind him.

"Don't forget to reset the alarm," she said.

He reset the alarm, dropped his briefcase on the hall table, loosened his tie, then sauntered into the living room. She followed. He turned. His gaze scanned her. Something hot and dark lit his blue eyes, something that stoked an answering heat in her.

With an arrogant quirk of his eyebrow, he gave her a slow, sizzling smile. "You look a little perturbed, Fortune. Not enjoying your stay? Accommodations not to your liking?"

She stalked toward him, not stopping until only inches separated them. "You jerk." She jabbed a finger into his chest, suppressing a wince when her finger connected with hard muscle. "How do you expect us to keep you safe if you can't be straight with us?"

He grabbed her hand and held it before she could poke him again. "What are you talking about?"

"You don't know?" she asked, jutting out her chin.

"Have no idea." He still held onto her hand.

She jerked free and stepped back. "You told us no one had keys to your place. What about Marissa?"

"Marissa?" He swiped a hand over his short hair. "I left her a message the other day telling her I wouldn't need her for awhile. That's why I didn't tell you. Did she show up here?"

"She sure did, cleaning products in hand."

"I didn't think she'd come. I didn't want to take any chance on her getting hurt while those thugs, or whoever, are out there. Maybe she never got the message." He narrowed his eyes. "You didn't hurt her, did you?"

"I didn't. But I scared the poor woman half to death. And I took her key away."

"You had no right to take the key. I trust her. I'll make sure she doesn't come back until this whole thing is over."

"I guarantee she won't come back. You lost your rights when those thugs threatened you. Right now, my job is to protect you and your job is to do what I say."

"No one tells me what to do."

"If you want to live, I'll tell you what to do. And you'll listen. 'Fess up. Now. Who else has a key to your place? And I hope you haven't given anyone your security code."

"There are people who have keys, people I trust. You don't need to know who they are. They won't come here until this mess is over."

Franco's cell phone rang. Frowning, he slipped the phone from his pocket and punched the connection to start the call. "Yeah?" he said roughly.

His face hardened as he listened for several seconds. "Who—" With a puzzled expression, he stared down at the phone, then slid it back into his pocket.

Her anger forgotten, Jo approached him. "It was him, wasn't it?"

He raised his gaze to hers. Fear and anger flashed in his eyes. "That sonofabitch." He headed toward the small bar. "I need a drink."

He grabbed two brandy snifters from the rack above the bar, plunked the glasses onto the wooden surface, and reached for a decanter filled with golden liquid. After pouring a shot into each glass, Franco came from behind the bar and held out a glass to Jo.

Shaking her head, she put up a hand.

"Take it. We both need a drink," he said.

"I don't drink when I'm on duty."

He set her glass on the bar. Jo watched the liquid swirl in the glass. Brandy always reminded her of her father. Memories, as warm as brandy, curled through her. Her dad had loved the sweet drink, and he'd loved her. Not so her stepfather. He'd enjoyed something much darker. A small shudder spilled over her warm memories.

Franco downed his drink in one swallow, then grabbed her glass from the bar.

Pushing aside her memories, good and bad, Jo caught his gaze. "Sit. We need to talk."

With a visible effort, Franco relaxed his shoulders and followed her to the sectional.

They sat down, and Jo kept what she hoped was a safe distance between them. Franco pulled his tie off, then threw it on the small table in front of the sofa. Still holding his brandy, he stared down at the liquid in his glass. Jo wished she could have some of the warming drink to chase the chills that had crept up her spine while she watched Franco's face as he'd listened to the call.

"What did he say?" she asked quietly.

He turned to her with expressionless eyes. "He knows Harris is my bodyguard and he knows the Town Car is bulletproof. Apparently, that angers him. He said no one will stop him from getting to me, and when he does, I either give him what he wants and he'll let me die quickly or he'll torture it out of me."

She shuddered. "And he wants money? Think, Franco. What money could he want?"

He knocked back his drink, set the empty glass on the table, then turned to her. "If I knew what he wanted, don't you think I'd give it to him?" His features tightened and he

27

looked away. "Money. Mac." He shook his head. "No, it couldn't be."

"Mac? What are you talking about?"

He looked at her. "It's nothing."

"Franco, you have to tell me everything."

"There's nothing to tell. I don't know why I thought of Mac. He's dead so he couldn't have anything to do with this."

Leaning back, she closed her eyes, taking large, even breaths, using the meditation technique one of her mental-health counselors had taught her. After the trauma of her childhood, then the Army and now the security firm, Jo had taught herself to stay calm in any circumstance, to isolate her emotions. The meditation worked its magic and soon blessed calm stole over her. She opened her eyes to Franco watching her.

"You okay?" he asked with a small smile. "I'm the one he wants to kill, not you."

"And I'm the one charged with keeping you alive."

His eyes softened and he reached for her, taking her hand in his. "Jo, it'll be okay."

She pulled away and scooted to the other end of the sofa. "It'll be okay so long as you listen to me and Harris, Callahan."

"It's Franco, remember?" He shot her a teasing grin that must have made countless women melt at his feet. She wasn't those other women. But the warmth that swirled through her told her she wasn't so different after all.

With a determined shove, she pushed up from her seat. "Stay here. I left my tablet in the kitchen. I have questions."

When she came back, Franco was lounging on the sofa, looking like a man without a care in the world. He'd lost the look of fear mixed with anger he'd had in his eyes when he'd hung up from the call. She wondered if years of partying had taught him how to mask his feelings, to put on the pretense of the international playboy. Jo suspected she might like the real Franco if he ever completely let down his guard. That frightened her almost as much as the thought of him being murdered.

Sinking down onto the cushions next to him, she turned on her tablet, then faced him.

"All business now, are we?" he said. "All right. Hit me with your questions."

"I need to satisfy my curiosity first." She scanned the elegantly decorated modern room. "The police report says your house was broken into two weeks ago. Sofa cushions ripped, tables overturned, drawers pulled out and emptied, food taken out of the refrigerator and thrown on the floor. Glasses and dishes broken." She swallowed the bile that rose in her throat. "And a death threat written in black marker on the living room wall. Is that right?"

"Don't forget the mattresses that were cut open."

Despite his nonchalant attitude, she'd seen the glint of fear in his eyes. "Yet, when I look around, this place is perfect. The upstairs is perfect. Your house looks like something out of a magazine."

"When you've got money, all it takes is a few phone calls—" he swept a hand out "— to end up with all this. Next question."

"Marissa said something about a lawyer you hired. She said she's legal, but was still afraid I was going to send her back to Mexico. What's going on, Franco?"

"Let it go, Josephine. It has nothing to do with what's happening now. Marissa's okay."

"I need to know everything about your life, Franco. You can't pick and choose what to tell us. Sometimes the smallest connection can unravel a bigger mystery. What are you into?"

"Next question."

He'd closed down. He was the most stubborn, hard-headed…

She sighed, knowing he had her in check. For now. "Who else has a key to your place?"

"Just some kids. They come in to water my plants, take out the garbage, things like that. I told them I don't need them for awhile."

"Kids? You hire kids to water your plants and take out your garbage? You can't even do that for yourself? And you gave them your key? How many kids? "

His lips tilted in one of his sexy smiles. "I can do a lot for myself. Care to find out?"

"Stop that. This is serious."

"I'm very serious," he said in a husky voice.

She ignored him and the warmth flooding her. Lowering her gaze, she entered her notes, then looked back up at him. "Who are these kids? I want names."

"The kids are okay. You'll have to trust me. I don't want them dragged into this. They won't come around again until it's safe, so don't worry about them. They've had it hard enough as it is."

Jo set the tablet on the table. "Damn it, Franco. Cooperate."

His jaw set in a stubborn line. "There are parts of my life that are off-limits to everyone, including you and my family."

Jo rubbed the back of her neck to ease the tension that

had taken root. "All right. I'm letting it go for now, but no one, and I mean no one—except you, me, and Harris—is to come in here until the cops find whoever's after you. And we need to change your locks."

"No need to change the locks. The kids and Marissa will stay away."

She leaned closer. "Locks get changed. And your back door too. We need a more secure door there."

He opened his mouth to say something, then clamped it shut.

"What aren't you telling me? You know I'll find out."

His eyes darkened and his features relaxed. "You want to know about me?" He reached for her and gently pulled her toward him.

She flattened her palms on his chest. "Of course, I—"

He touched the mole on her left cheek. "Your beauty mark is a real turn-on."

"It's a mole."

"On you, it's sexy as hell."

Before she knew it, his lips were over hers, soft at first, then more demanding. He tasted like brandy and aroused male. She stiffened even as a low moan escaped from her. Heat centered in her stomach and flared outward. Anxiety, unwanted but always present, reared up, diffusing the heat. She couldn't do this. Not with this man. She pushed away from him, her breathing ragged.

Wiping her hand across her mouth, she rasped, "Still the player, I see."

CHAPTER FOUR

Franco stared at Jo's retreating back as she bolted from the room. The woman had him reeling. She'd wanted him. There'd been no mistaking her response to his kiss. But when she'd pulled away, her eyes had glittered with fear, a fear he knew too well. He'd seen that look before, more times than he'd care to admit. It couldn't be. Stress must be playing with his mind. Jo was too tough. His imagination was in overdrive. And yet...

He leaned his head back and closed his eyes.

He wanted her. And Franco Callahan always got what he wanted. But if what he suspected was true, he'd have to be careful, go easy with her, bring her around slowly. He would never hurt Jo. If he'd read the look in her eyes right, she'd been hurt enough.

"Most of my clients would kill for your hair." Anita Santisi, Franco's cousin and one of Philadelphia's top hair stylists, loosened Jo's hair from its braid and fluffed it out until it streamed down Jo's back. Feeling out of her element in the upscale surroundings of Anita's hair salon, Jo shifted uncomfortably in one of the large chairs. She glanced around, anything to avoid the wall of mirrors that reflected her very real discomfort. The bustling salon was filled this morning with sophisticated women dressed in the latest casual fashions. Somehow, even wearing kimonos over their clothes, with dye on their hair or sitting under dryers wearing plastic caps, the women projected high chic. Flashes of gold and diamonds on fingers and wrists peeked from the sleeves of the dark gray kimonos. Anita's staff, men and women alike, was young and beautiful and dressed in head-to-toe black.

Anita had been welcoming and friendly since Harris had dropped Jo off at the shop fifteen minutes ago. With her edgy sophistication and sexy clothes, Anita had always rubbed Jo the wrong way. While Anita and Doriana resembled each other with their thick black hair and large gold-brown eyes, Doriana was softly sweet to Anita's sharp angles. Now Jo saw that despite Anita's brazen sexuality, her eyes were sad. Jo knew little about Anita's personal life except that a man had once hurt her badly. Maybe she and Anita had more in common than anyone would think.

Jo sighed. Focusing on Anita diverted her from the real purpose of her visit. She was here to get glammed up. She hated that expression. Drawing on the well of pride that had always been the source of her defense, she pushed aside her misgivings and stole a glance in the mirror. She seldom wore her hair down. The sunlight streaming through the large windows highlighted the golden strands in her wildly flowing red hair. She wouldn't admit it to anyone, but she'd always been a tad vain about her hair.

"Girl, you are going to look ravishing when I'm done with you," Anita said.

Jo caught Anita's gaze in the mirror and shot her an ironic look. "You'd have to be a miracle worker to do that." She grabbed the mug of coffee from the worktable in front of her, needing a little caffeine sustenance.

Anita frowned. "Why do you say that? You're gorgeous with those green eyes and high cheekbones. I'm only enhancing nature. You're going to drive Franco crazy. I can't wait to see my arrogant cousin taken down a notch or two."

Widening her eyes, Jo nearly dropped her mug onto the Formica counter. "I'm not here to drive him crazy. I'm here to…you know why." Franco had already explained Jo's presence to his cousin. Anita was family and could be trusted.

Anita came around to face her, leaning her hip against the counter. "Seriously, Jo, there isn't a part of you that wants to see the man squirm? The times we've been together at family gatherings, you and Franco are like two sparks, ready to flare up the minute you touch." She laughed softly. "Or like two cats hissing at each other."

She gave Jo a self-satisfied smile. "You two don't fool me one bit. Why do you think I'm so successful? I can read people. You are going to have my cousin worshipping at your feet when we're done with you. The man's already got a thing for you."

Jo laughed at the absurdity of it all. "Please, Anita. I am in no way Franco's type."

"You think not? Girl, open your eyes."

"They are very open to how Franco feels about me." She lowered her gaze. Anita had hit on a partial truth. When Franco had kissed her yesterday, a part of her had been tempted to give in to the curiosity that had eaten away at her from the first time she'd met him. But fear had reared up as always, pounding in her chest, driving her away. Franco was dangerous. He made her want something she'd long ago decided she didn't need.

Anita's soft laugh cut into Jo's gloomy thoughts. "You'll admit soon enough you and Franco have something going on. Now, let's wash this hair and I'll work my magic, although it is a shame to trim even a little of it."

Twenty minutes later a new kind of anxiety wound through Jo while Anita snipped her hair. As large swatches of her damp hair fell to the floor, an overwhelming urge to run out of the shop hit Jo. She gripped the chair arms.

"You look scared to death," Anita said. "Trust me. You're going to love your hair when I'm finished."

Jo forced herself to relax. "It's just that in the last sixteen years, since I was seventeen, I've only had my hair trimmed a few times. In the Army I was allowed to keep it long, but I had to wear it in a tight bun."

"You're not seventeen or in the Army now, girlfriend. You're a grown woman. You wouldn't want to be seventeen again. It's not a good age, at least not in my family." Anita shook her head. "Doriana got pregnant with Josh when she was seventeen, and Franco got himself into big trouble when he was that age. Even Uncle Dan couldn't get him out of it."

Jo's gaze met Anita's in the mirror. "What kind of trouble?"

"The usual kid stuff, but it wasn't the first time he'd gotten into trouble. Uncle Dan's money and influence got him out of it the other times. Let Franco tell you if he wants." She stopped snipping, a thoughtful look on her face. "Franco was the sweetest little boy even though Doriana and I teased him mercilessly. She's four years older than him and I'm three. Something changed when he became a teen. Got smartass and arrogant. Maybe it was because Aunt Lena and Uncle Dan spoiled him. The Italian-Irish prince. And he stayed arrogant and smartass until Uncle Dan had the stroke. We're all shocked at how Franco finally manned up and put himself on the right track." She shrugged. "Guess he had it in him all along."

◇◇◇

Jo blinked several times and looked into the mirror again. Yup! That was her staring back. She touched her hair, running her fingers through the shoulder length cut. The layering brought out the golden highlights and framed her eyes. And the makeup Anita had applied made her skin glow and covered up the sprinkling of freckles on her nose. Her eyes looked wider and greener now, and the subtle rose-colored blush brought out her high cheekbones. Never having taken the time to learn to apply makeup, Jo had eschewed it.

Anita's smiling staff gathered around her, oohhing and aahhing.

"I can't believe the change in you," one of the shampoo girls said, awe in her voice.

"You are absolutely beautiful," one of the stylists said.

Jo flushed at their compliments. She must look like a Christmas bulb with her red face and her red hair.

Anita studied her. "Jo, you are one of the most beautiful women I've ever seen."

"You did it, Anita."

The other woman shook her head. "I had a lot to work with." She nodded toward the small bag resting on the counter. "All the products you need are in there. You remember how to use the makeup and style your hair?"

Jo nodded.

"Okay, then, but if you ever need help with any of that, call me." Anita's gaze swept Jo. "Time to burn those fatigues and have you looking like a real girl. Come on, let's go next door."

Jo groaned, making the women around her laugh. Mitzi, the owner of the boutique next to the salon was a personal shopper. She'd offered to outfit Jo in some new clothes now, then take her shopping tomorrow at Neiman Marcus to choose an entire wardrobe. Franco had insisted on paying for everything. Embarrassment at the thought of him buying her clothes, including lingerie, warred with indignation. The idea of Franco, or any man, buying her clothes made her feel like a kept woman. No, she wouldn't go there. She wasn't anyone's woman. She'd been on her own since she was eighteen, and she could take care of herself. At least he hadn't insisted on coming shopping with them.

Plastering a smile on her face, she waved goodbye to the others in the shop and followed Anita out the door to the boutique, her mind awhirl. Franco was picking her up in two hours to take her to dinner. Their farce would begin tonight. Not for the first time she wondered if she'd been too hasty to agree to this whole masquerade. She'd never convince anyone that handsome, rich Franco Callahan could be in love with someone like her.

Two hours later Jo stood in Anita's now-closed shop and smoothed her hands down the sides of her short black dress. The dress flared around her thighs, giving her movement. She'd insisted on that. Above that, though, the stretchy material clung to every curve, making her feel exposed, vulnerable. With each new piece of clothing she'd slipped on she'd felt like she'd lost a little of herself, lost the armor that had protected her all these years.

She tugged on the hem of her dress again and looked down at the strappy black high-heeled sandals she wore. The sexy shoes were surprisingly comfortable, and with her good sense of balance, she'd gotten used to the high heels much quicker than she would have imagined. A part of her longed for her sturdy, familiar combat boots. Wearing fatigues and boots felt right. The slinky black dress and high heels didn't. At least the silly little jewel-encrusted purse she carried was large enough to hold her gun, in addition to her lipstick, a comb, and her phone.

"Stop trying to pull down your dress," Anita said beside her. "You look amazing. Who knew under those fatigues and T-shirts was a sexy woman with a great body? You'll floor Franco."

"I told you I'm here to do a job. I don't care what Franco thinks of my disguise." But a part of her did. The low neckline of the dress and the lacy push-up bra made her breasts look bigger. She hated to admit it, but she felt sexy. Jo knew she had a good body. She worked out and kept in shape.

"You're just what Franco needs," Anita said.

Jo's response drifted away as the Town Car eased up to the curb out front and Harris jumped out, then opened the door for Franco. Dressed in a dark blue suit that fit him as if it were tailor-made, which, Jo decided, it probably had been, and with his hair slicked back, Franco's elegant look spoke of a world where she didn't belong.

She yanked on the hem of her dress.

Anita slapped Jo's hand. "Stop fooling with the dress," she said as she hurried to unlock the door for the men.

"Hey, cuz," Franco said, sliding in and giving Anita a light kiss on the cheek. Harris gave Anita a curt hello before she closed the door behind them.

Franco slid his glance to Jo and froze. His brow furrowed, then his gaze made a slow trip down her body and back to her face. His eyes grew dark and hot. He walked toward her, then took one of her hands in his. He lifted her hand and turned it over, brushing a soft kiss on her wrist. Her skin tingled where he touched. He leaned toward her and whispered in her ear, "I like your hair. You look amazing."

He was focused on her like a laser. Jo felt the rest of the world fade away as his eyes devoured her. No wonder he had so many beautiful women after him. She wanted to shoot back with a smart retort but words dried in her throat.

He smiled as if he could read her thoughts. "First time I've ever known you to be speechless, Fortune."

His teasing tone broke through the spell he'd held her in. "Don't get too used to it, Callahan."

He laughed. "That's my Jo. I knew you were in there somewhere."

Heat suffused her cheeks and she lowered her eyes.

"I guess you'd better get going." Anita strode to the reception desk and grabbed the shopping bags holding Jo's products and the new clothes. "Don't forget these." She handed the bags to Harris. "And, Jo, your wrap." She snatched the silk shawl from the counter. The delicate shawl, in iridescent shades of green and gold, shimmered like dragonfly wings.

Franco took the wrap from Anita and placed it over Jo's shoulders, unobtrusively sliding his fingers down her arms in a delicious caress that left a trail of fire in their wake. Grasping her small jeweled purse like a lifeline in one hand, Jo took the arm Franco offered.

"Just a minute." Anita stepped toward them and fluffed Jo's hair around her face. She leaned close to whisper in Jo's ear. "Remember what I said. The man practically melted when he saw you. You've got the power."

CHAPTER FIVE

The elegant restaurant fell into a hush when they walked in. Diners, some discreet, others more brazen, craned their necks to watch Jo and Franco as they wove their way between white-clothed tables. Previously a bank, the large room, dominated by graceful marble columns and brass accents, had an Old World feel. Soft lighting swathed the room in romantic shadows. It was clear Franco frequented the restaurant. He called the maitre d´ by name and nodded to a few people seated at the tables. Most of the patrons looked quickly away when Jo's gaze met theirs. But others assessed her with bold looks, especially the women. To her surprise quite a few men sent her admiring glances.

Franco put his hand on Jo's waist as they followed Maurice, the maitre d´, to a small table tucked into a corner. When Maurice pulled out a chair that would have her sitting with her back to the room, she shook her head and indicated the other chair, the one where she had a full view of the room. Maurice graciously pulled out the chair she wanted and she sat. Franco sat across from her. With a smile and a flourish, the maitre d´ handed them menus printed on heavy vellum and left.

Jo opened her menu and scanned the selections. Her eyes widened. There weren't any prices. She'd heard of restaurants like this, where the women's menus didn't show the prices. It would be nice for a change to order whatever she wanted and not worry about the cost.

"See anything you like?" Franco asked.

She glanced at him over the top of the menu. "Most of the entrees seem to be steak."

He laughed. "It is a steakhouse after all."

"That explains it." She chewed her lip, studying the menu. "Maybe a filet mignon? I'm not sure."

"I eat here often. Okay with you if I order for both of us? Or do you want to be in control of the food too?" His teasing tone softened his words and made her smile.

"Sure," she said with a shrug. "This is your field of expertise. Remember that security is mine. Quit fighting me and let me do my job."

"Aye, aye, captain."

She resisted the urge to roll her eyes.

After the wine steward took their drink order, Franco signaled their waiter that they were ready to order. "Filet for both of us, Paolo, the way I always have it."

While they waited for their food, they sipped their drinks—Franco, a deep red cabernet, and Jo, sparkling water.

She took a long sip of the refreshing water and carefully scanned the large room. Everything seemed normal. She breathed a little easier, but didn't let up her guard. When she set the crystal goblet on the table and raised her eyes, Franco was staring at her over the rim of his glass. His intense gaze made Jo touch her mouth, wondering if she had crumbs on her face from the delicious hot roll she'd eaten. "What?"

With a smile, Franco set down his glass, reached across the table, and touched the tip of her nose. "I like the new look, but I miss the freckles. I'm glad you didn't cover up the beauty mark."

41

"It's a mole."

He laughed.

She fidgeted over the admiration in his eyes, his admiration a double-edged sword. What he liked wasn't really her. She wanted him to like the real Jo, not this glamorous imitation.

She pulled her wrap tighter across her shoulders, hiding the new façade and maybe even her foolish pride. Franco knew how to push her buttons, make her react, yet it was all an act. She was someone with a skill set he needed—for awhile. When this case was over, they'd go their separate ways again. Until then the case was her focus. Nothing else.

"We have some business to discuss," she said.

"You're going to ruin a great dinner with business?"

"When it means your safety, yes."

"Care about me that much, Fortune?"

"Just doing my job."

"What do you want to talk about?" His features tensed. "And if it's about the door, forget it. We argued about it enough last night. I'm not changing it."

"I've already contacted a company about switching the back door to a steel one."

He picked up his wine goblet and finished off his drink. The wine steward hurried over and refilled the glass.

Franco's gaze held hers. "My house is over one hundred years old. I can do what I want with the interior, but the exterior has to keep its historic character. I don't want the historical society on my butt."

"You've got a lot more problems than a snooty historical society. My job is to keep you alive. Someone broke in through the back door before and they can do it again. We'll store the door in the basement until you're safe again, then you can switch it back. And if your neighbors complain, tell them to go pound sand."

"Easy for you to say. I have to live with these people. And I like my door."

"Too bad. It's getting changed."

He stared at her for long seconds, and she suspected he fought with himself. Then his features relaxed. "I can see I'm losing this round."

She traced her fingers over the rivulets of cool water running down the sides of her goblet. He was finally getting that she knew best how to protect him. "I'll set up the appointment for the door for day after tomorrow. I'd have the door done tomorrow, but I have to meet with Anita's friend Mitzi and go shopping for a new wardrobe." She rolled her eyes. "Your protection is more important than my clothes, Franco. I think I should postpone the shopping trip until the new door is in."

"No. We agreed. You want to carry this masquerade off, you dress the part."

"My point exactly. We're both making concessions here."

Sipping his wine, he leaned back in his chair. "As part of the deal, I'll give in about the door. I have a security system now. Go on your shopping trip. One more day with the old door won't hurt."

"I still can't believe you didn't have a security system in that expensive house until after someone broke in."

"And I can't believe you don't want to go shopping for new clothes. You look amazing tonight."

"Don't change the subject. These clothes are not me."

"Yes, they are. You just don't want to admit how sexy you are. Every man in this room wishes you were with him.

Didn't you see the looks you got when we came in?"

She had, but wouldn't admit it to him. "That wasn't for me. That was curiosity to see who you had with you."

"Sweetheart, trust me. The guys were checking you out. I'm the envy of every guy here."

He sounded proud to be with her. She took a long swig of her drink, as if she could swallow away the pleasure that thought gave her.

"The clothes are yours," she said, setting down her empty glass. "You're paying for them. When this case is over, I'm leaving them with you. You know I have an expense account."

"I don't want Logan's money. The clothes are my gift to you. Take them."

"I don't want anything from you. Besides, I'm more comfortable in my fatigues."

"I don't believe that," he said. "I think you know how terrific you look tonight, and I think you like it."

She drummed her fingers on the table, unwilling to acknowledge the truth of his words, even to herself.

He reached over and took one of her hands in his, studying it, then he rubbed a finger over the thin scars on her knuckles. "Did you get these in the line of duty?"

"One of the perks of the job."

He turned her hand over and made circles on her palm with his finger. Delicious shivers ran up her arm.

Franco's eyes softened. "Jo, what are you afraid of? You hide behind those unflattering fatigues as if you're scared to let anyone see how beautiful you are and what a perfect body you have. Don't hide yourself anymore. Be proud of who you are."

Lowering her gaze, she took shallow breaths. He'd figured her out. Unacceptable.

"Jo?"

She gathered her courage and met his gaze.

"You can tell me anything," he said. "I won't hurt you. I'd never hurt you."

"End of conversation." She pulled free.

"Damn it, Jo," he said in a soft voice.

Wanting to flee the table, the restaurant, his knowing gaze, she looked away, and noticed a stunning blonde heading toward them with determined strides. Jo sat straighter, her attention zeroed, laser-like, on the blonde. Beautiful didn't mean harmless.

With a rustle of silk and a whiff of expensive perfume, the woman reached their table and looked down at them. In a heavily accented voice, she intoned, "If it isn't Franco Callahan."

Wearing a skintight white dress that left little to the imagination and sky-high gold sandals, the blonde stood well over six feet tall. Her straight hair flowed past her waist.

Franco cleared his throat and stood up. "Elise. Good to see you again."

"Don't give me that *merde,*" the blonde said.

The blonde was probably French, judging from the accent and the French word for shit.

"You promised to call me," the French woman said. "That was over six months ago. And what do I hear from you? Nothing."

"I didn't promise to call," Franco said. "I told you I'd try. I'm very busy at work. You know that."

The other woman looked down at Jo, seeming to notice her for the first time. "Is this your work?" Her icy blue eyes looked Jo up and down. "You like little redheads now?" Disdain dripped from her voice.

Franco blew out a breath. "Elise, this is Jo. And this is not a place to discuss our differences."

The blonde's gaze met Jo's. "Don't trust this piece of excrement. He'll say anything to get into your bed." She turned back to Franco and ran her hand over his lapel. "But he's worth it. Call me, Franco," she said in a sultry purr.

Franco's hands clenched at his sides and a muscle twitched in his jaw. Amused to see his discomfort, Jo stifled a laugh.

The waiter came just then with their food, putting an end to the little tableau.

"You'll have to excuse us, Elise," Franco said. "And by the way, I'm with Jo now, and that's where I want to be."

Jo blinked at his words. With effort, she reminded herself Franco was playing a part. That was all. And she'd do well to remember that.

The joy the evening had engendered in her heart dissolved.

◇◇◇

"That was delicious." Jo let out a satisfied sigh and leaned back in her chair. "I've never tasted such a tender steak. I could cut it with a butter knife. And that seasoning was to die for."

Franco smiled. "I knew you'd like the wild porcini rub."

"It was exquisite."

His smile faded and his eyes darkened. Moving closer, he touched her hand where it rested on the table. "You're exquisite. I enjoyed watching you enjoy the meal."

"Don't do that." She slipped her hand from his and gathered her purse from the table. "While you pay the bill,

I'll call Harris and tell him we're ready."

"Yes, ma'am."

Shaking her head at his words and his teasing grin, she pulled out her phone and punched in Harris' number.

A short while later, Jo's wrap slipped from her shoulders as she and Franco stood just inside the restaurant waiting for Harris. With a gentle touch, Franco adjusted her wrap. His fingers slid over her nape in a soft caress that sent delicious heat over her nerve endings to settle in a knot of desire low in her belly. She stepped away from him and the enticement he offered.

"I wonder what's keeping Harris. He should have been here by now," she said. "He was only parked around the corner."

"Probably got caught at a light." Franco took a deep breath. "It's a nice night. After that meal, I could use a walk. Why don't we go down the street? He'll see us."

"Nope. We're staying right here."

"Don't be a wuss. I thought you were tough."

"Nice try. Insults don't work with me. We don't move until we see the car. It's awfully quiet out there." Jo opened her bag and slid out her gun, discreetly holding it at her side. "Stay here." She stepped outside and peeked from the canopy covering the doorway. Elegant shops featuring beautiful clothes and upscale home furnishings lined the trendy street, deserted now. As quaint as the street was, she would have felt more secure if the restaurant was on one of the city's main thoroughfares.

A black Town Car slid down the street. Jo breathed a sigh of relief and waited for Harris to pull up in front of the restaurant. She signaled to Franco, gazing from behind the glass doors, to stay where he was. Once she knew everything was safe, he could come out.

Gun drawn as a precaution, she scanned the street as she walked toward the car. But instead of Harris, two men, large, brawny, their faces shaded by caps, jumped out of the vehicle. They halted when they saw her and lifted their own guns.

"Get back in the car and drive away and no one gets hurt," she said in a steely voice.

"Your one gun can't stop our two. How about you and Callahan get into the car and we all drive away nice," the larger of the two guys growled.

"Not happening," Jo said.

"We're not going anywhere," Franco said, coming up behind her.

She had no more time to think as the first guy rushed her. Adrenaline pumping, Jo kicked off her high heels. She jumped and twisted, kicking the gun out of his hand, then slammed her own gun against his head.

"What the—?" Bleeding, he grabbed for her.

"Leave her—" Franco's words were cut short when thug number two hit him on the head with the butt of his gun. He caught Franco under the arms as he went down, preparing to push Franco into the car.

The thug closest to Jo widened his eyes as her right foot connected with his groin. When he doubled over, she whacked him on the head again with her gun.

Franco's thug let him drop to the ground and turned his gun on Jo. Screams came from up the street, then the sounds of running feet slapping the sidewalk. Apparently changing his mind, Franco's thug bolted for the car. Hers, still holding his crotch, yanked open the back door and dove in. With the door still swinging wide, the car careened down the street.

Franco had regained his feet but reeled slightly, blood dripping from a cut over his eyebrow. Jo grabbed his arm, steadying him. Their Town Car sped toward them. When the car came to a screeching stop, Harris jumped out.

"I'm sorry," he said. "Someone put up construction barriers that closed off the streets and I couldn't—"

"It's okay," Jo said, interrupting him. "Later. Help me get Franco into the car."

A small group of bystanders had gathered nearby. "I called 9-1-1," a man said.

Harris looked up from settling Franco into the back-seat. "Thanks, but we can't stick around. We need to get our friend to the hospital."

Jo grabbed her shoes, wrap and purse where she'd dropped them on the sidewalk and slid in beside Franco. Harris slammed the door shut, then got into the driver's seat and sped away.

"No hospital," Franco said, rubbing his temple. Blood came off on his fingers.

"Yes, hospital," Jo said. "And don't ever disobey my orders again. I told you to stay inside."

He reached out and touched her face. She felt his warm blood on her skin.

"You were magnificent," he said just before he lost consciousness.

Jo settled him against her, cradling his head under her chin.

"Hurry," she said to Harris.

CHAPTER SIX

The sound of shattering glass followed by the loud blare of the security alarm jerked Jo's attention from her laptop on the kitchen's center island. As she grabbed her gun from the counter and sprang to her feet, the stool she'd been sitting on clattered onto the tile floor. She whirled and scanned the kitchen. Everything intact. The digital clock on the microwave said three a.m.

Gun in hand, she raced into the dining room, adjacent to the kitchen, and slid to a halt. Shards of glass sprinkled over the Oriental carpet. A large rock, the size of a baseball, lay among the glass shards. The gaping hole in one of the small multi-panes stared at her like a one-eyed monster.

She ran back into the kitchen, stood to one side of the back door and peered out the window. After a quick perusal of the small backyard, she flipped the latch, flung the door open and hurried outside. Moonlight illuminated the flagstone patio with its wrought iron chairs and table and the tiny garden beyond with its brick path winding through rose bushes to a high wooden fence. The elaborate iron gate to the alleyway was swinging open. Her sneakers slapped the brick as she sprinted to the gate. She knew before she got to the alleyway that whoever had thrown that rock was long gone.

"Jo!"

She turned at Franco's voice. Outlined in the dim light

from the kitchen, he stood in the doorway, clad only in tapered boxers.

"Get back in the house," she yelled, dashing toward him. "Are you crazy?"

"Are you okay?" he asked, rushing out to meet her.

"Don't worry about me." She grabbed his arm and pulled him into the house, then slammed the door and locked it.

Breathing heavily, adrenaline rushing through her veins, she scanned his nearly naked self. "You walked over glass in your bare feet?"

"I'm fine. Are you okay? You're the one who's crazy running out there like that. Whoever did this could still be outside."

"It's my job to protect you. I'm not afraid and I have my gun."

The blaring alarm suddenly ceased. The silence was almost eerie, their harsh breathing the only sounds in the room. The alarm must have reset itself. "Did the security company call?"

He nodded. "They're sending the police." He pointed into the dining room. "Was that a rock I saw lying on the carpet?"

"Yup. What is this, the Middle Ages? Who does that?"

"Some very determined people," he said quietly.

"You should be in bed." Her gaze went to the butterfly bandage above his right eyebrow. "You only got back from the ER two hours ago."

"I'm fine. What are you doing up at this hour?"

"It's called round-the-clock protection. Harris relieves me at five."

"I don't like it. I have the alarm now. There's no reason

51

for you to stay up."

"I don't tell you how to do your job so don't tell me how to do mine. Now get dressed before the police get here."

Despite the seriousness of the situation, she couldn't help but notice how his bare chest looked like marble—sculpted, muscled, and beautiful. His athletic legs were long and perfectly formed, the muscles defined. "I mean it. Get dressed. Now. And put some shoes on."

His eyes turned to steel. Franco Callahan clearly didn't like taking orders from anyone. With his mouth set in a grim line, he turned and headed out of the room.

Detective Dave Morelli of the Philadelphia police snapped his notebook closed and slipped it into the inside pocket of his suit jacket, then stood. "We've got all we need. We'll get the note and the rock to the lab. Hopefully, they'll be able to pull off some prints."

Wearing latex gloves, he unfurled the piece of paper and looked down at it. "This is some serious business," he said, then read the note aloud again. "*This is your last warning. Give us the money or the girlfriend dies.*" The detective slipped the note into the plastic bag one of the uniformed cops handed him, then pulled off his gloves and stuffed them into his pocket.

"Thanks for everything, Detective." Franco stood, too, and the men shook hands.

Jo pushed up from the sectional and thrust out her hand to the detective. He shook it, then nodded. "Glad Mr. Callahan has protection. You'll let us know if anything else happens?"

"Sure will, Detective," she said. "I'll fill in my boss and the other bodyguard. And you'll keep us informed if you learn anything?"

"I will." With a nod, Morelli headed toward the door with the two uniformed officers. He and the cops slipped out the door and Franco locked it after them, then reset the alarm.

He turned to Jo and rubbed a hand over his hair, still mussed from sleep. Dressed in jeans and a T-shirt, and with dark stubble on his face and the small butterfly bandage, he was the sexiest guy she'd ever known. She looked down at the floor. She had to get a grip. The man could make her forget everything she'd learned about control, about taking charge of a situation.

He moved closer until inches separated them. He didn't touch her. "It's almost five. Harris will be here soon. Why don't you go up to bed, get some rest?"

Clearing her throat, she stepped back. "You're the one who needs rest. Remember getting cracked on the head? The pain, the ER?"

"I'm too wound up to sleep. Do you want coffee, tea, warm milk, anything?"

She shook her head. "Franco, you really need to rest. And we need to call someone to fix the window. Then we get that kitchen door changed today. The back of your house is too exposed with that alleyway."

He winced and touched his injured temple. "I've agreed to change the door, but this time they didn't use the door, did they?"

"No, but that doesn't mean they won't try it again."

Releasing a resigned sigh, he said, "I'll call the window people when I get to work. The window is a historic design and there's only one company in Philadelphia that can duplicate the glass."

"The doctor said you need to stay in bed for a day. You're not going anywhere."

"I've just got a headache. I'll be fine. I have a company to run and the gun didn't do any real damage. Simmer down, Fortune."

"You could have been killed last night." The thought shook her. She slid her gaze away, hiding her feelings from him, and ran a hand over her denim-clad thigh. The feel of the rough fabric calmed her. "You should have stayed in the restaurant like I told you."

"Jo, look at me."

When she turned back to him, he framed her face between his strong hands. "You're right. I should have listened to you. But I couldn't let you face those thugs alone." He held her gaze. His lips quirked. "I know I'm a stubborn ass at times."

She laughed, releasing the tension tightening every one of her muscles. "Try all the time."

His eyes gleamed with mischief. "Then you'll have to work harder to keep me in line. And I promise to fight you every step of the way."

He rubbed his thumbs over her cheekbones, then stopped as if he realized what he was doing. Their eyes met and she held her breath as he bent forward and brushed his lips gently over hers. She tensed, holding herself rigid, but he continued to kiss her, sweetly, with tenderness, until she began to melt around the edges. With a low moan, she returned his kiss. Her resistance dissolved like mist under a hot sun and she opened to him. Their tongues danced for several charged minutes, then Franco pulled away.

Her eyes snapped open.

His eyes, blue velvet, looked deeply into hers. "That

wasn't so bad, was it?"

Dazed, she touched her lips, but no words would come.

He gathered her to him, tucking her head under his chin.

Without thinking, she wrapped her arms around his waist. She felt serene for the first time in a very long while. She could stand on her own, always had. Surely, it wouldn't hurt to allow herself to be comforted, if only for a little while. She should be soothing Franco. He'd been hurt last night. He could have been killed. Yet, he was the one comforting her. She snuggled closer. The man had unexpected depths. The playboy she could handle. This new Franco held more danger.

A heavy dose of reality intruded and she pulled away. A glance at the wall clock told her it was five o'clock. The world was waking up.

"You can't go to work today," she said. "Rest. We'll take care of the window and the new door."

"I have to go to work. I've got a big meeting with an important client. My staff's put in a lot of work. I can't let them down." He headed toward the foyer, then turned around, frowning. He crossed the space between them.

"I had something I wanted to say." He touched her lips with his fingers. "But you distracted me."

"What?" Anxiety and the heat of his touch sent hot-cold shivers up her arms.

"That note made up my mind about something." He took one of her hands in his. "Those creeps made a direct threat against you. It's no longer just about me. They've got it in for you too."

"They won't get to me. That was posturing to scare you."

"I won't let anything happen to you," he said, his voice low and even. "I'm calling Logan today and having you taken off the case. You're not safe here."

Anger shot through her with the speed of a bullet and she yanked free. "You. Will. Not call Logan and tell him I can't do my job."

"That's not what I meant. I...Jo, why do you hire yourself out like this?"

She glared at him. "You make me sound like a prostitute. I help people. I keep them safe when they're threatened. It's what I do."

He backed up and straightened. "I didn't mean to offend you. I admire what you do, Jo. I do. I just...I don't want you hurt."

"I can take care of myself, Callahan. I don't need you or anyone else to worry about me."

A knock sounded at the door. "There's Harris," she snapped.

Then strode to the door, feeling totally unprofessional.

CHAPTER SEVEN

After the glass people replaced the broken window and the door company installed the new steel back door, Jo snagged a few hours sleep, but it didn't help much. Even three cups of coffee couldn't clear the cobwebs in her head. The quiet of the house pressed around her as she searched the refrigerator and freezer for tonight's dinner. After the night and morning she and Franco had endured, Jo craved comfort food and needed some major de-stressing. She'd make Franco stay home tonight and rest. If he even dared try to go out, she'd hog-tie him and sit on him. A small chuckle escaped her as she imagined how well that would go over with him.

Franco had a well-stocked pantry and refrigerator, surprising for a bachelor. She didn't like to admit it, but she enjoyed cooking and was pretty good at it. She dug a container of spaghetti sauce out of the freezer, along with a small loaf of Italian bread, then found a package of pasta in the pantry. Add a salad and garlic bread, and they'd have a decent meal. She glanced at the clock. Almost five. Franco should be home soon. He'd promised to cut his hours short today.

She'd defrost the sauce in the microwave to cut down on time, then heat it on the stove. While the water boiled for the pasta and the sauce heated she'd make the salad and prepare the garlic bread. She felt calmer already.

Her cell phone rang. She slid it from the pocket of her

fatigues. Harris' number blinked on her screen. "Hey," she said into the phone. "You guys on your way?"

"Well," he drawled. "Not yet. Our man has decided he needs a workout. I'm drivin' him to the gym. I'll get him home in a few hours."

"Harris, for God's sake, Franco was attacked last night. He needs to rest, not go to the gym."

"I know, darlin', but the man's head is harder than one of those cement pilings stuck in the Delaware. I'll call you when we're on our way from the gym." He chuckled. "What time should Brewer pick you up tomorrow for your shopping excursion?" Brewer, a security expert and ex-SEAL friend of Harris, would guard Jo and Mitzi when they shopped.

Jo wrinkled her nose. "How about ten?" She hated the thought of a full day of shopping. And now that she'd been threatened, she needed her own security when she left the house. That sucked too. Brewer would drive Mitzi and her to the upscale King of Prussia mall and stay with them.

After ending the call, she hoisted herself onto one of the high stools surrounding the center island. No sense starting dinner yet. With a little time on her hands, she decided to make a note of everything that had happened to Franco in the last few weeks. He might not realize it, but he held the key to whoever was threatening him. She had to force him to think, really think, about who might want him dead.

Two hours later, as the aroma of tomato and basil from the sauce simmering on the stove wafted over the kitchen, Jo inhaled the calming, homey scent while she filled a large pot with water and placed it on the stove. She'd made a large salad, enough for at least four. Hopefully she'd convince Harris to stay and eat with them. She enjoyed the older man's company, and his presence would help diffuse the sexual tension that always heated the air around Franco and her.

She'd reached for the knob to ignite the burner under the pot when the doorbell rang. Jo froze. Dread pumped through her. Harris hadn't called yet to say they were on the way, and he and Franco would never ring the bell. Pulse racing, she grabbed her gun from the counter and headed for the front door. Damn historical society with their restrictions. Franco's house needed security cameras front and back.

She approached the door cautiously and looked through the peephole, then released an agitated breath. Lena and Dan Callahan stood outside. What were Franco's parents doing here? She put the gun behind her in the waistband of her pants and disengaged the security alarm, then opened the door. She glanced quickly around. The street was deserted.

"Lena and Dan, what a nice surprise." Jo moved aside to let them in. It wasn't safe for any of them to stand outside for too long.

Lena, slender and sophisticated, greeted Jo with a big smile. "Jo, how nice to see you again."

"You too," Jo said, with another nervous glance outside. "Come in."

Dan, his hair now completely gray, leaned on a cane and nodded at her. While Lena helped Dan into the house, Jo bit back her impatience, her attention glued to the street as she held the door open. If anyone was out there…

When the older couple was finally inside, Jo hurriedly locked the door, then leaned against it. By the frightened look on Lena's face, Jo knew she'd noticed the gun when Jo turned to close the door.

"Go on into the living room," Jo said. She needed to get Franco's parents' thoughts away from the blatant reminder of their son's troubles. While they headed into the living room, Jo reset the security alarm.

Lena chewed her lip but said nothing as she took her husband's elbow and helped him into the other room.

Pity stirred in Jo as she watched Dan's shuffle. He was far from the vibrant corporate mogul she'd first met five years ago. The stroke had taken its toll, making Dan's speech difficult and his gait slow. But physical therapy helped, and Lena constantly hovered like a mother hen. Dan's mind was still sharp, though. Franco sent him weekly reports on the company's dealings and Dan offered Franco advice, whether Franco wanted it or not.

Lena settled Dan into a chair then turned to Jo. She looked Jo up and down, her brown eyes assessing. "I love what Anita did with your hair. It shows off your beautiful face."

"Thanks, Lena." Jo ran a hand over her hair and looked away, suddenly uncomfortable. She'd never learned how to accept compliments.

"You are getting rid of those fatigues, right?"

At Lena's question, Jo turned to her and bit back a smile. Lena's forthrightness she could handle. Better than the compliments, anyway.

"I'm getting rid of the fatigues for the time being." She gestured to the chair next to Dan's. "Why don't you sit too? Franco should be home soon. I expect his driver to call any minute. Do you want anything to drink? Tea, coffee, wine? I've got dinner cooking. Will you and Dan stay?"

Where had that come from? Domestic she was not. Yet, here she was offering drinks and asking them to stay for dinner. What was next? Wearing aprons? Cutting out coupons?

Lena dropped her purse on the floor, slipped off her leather jacket and laid it over the arm of the chair, then sat.

"I'll have some wine. Thanks." She turned to her husband. "Dinner sounds wonderful, doesn't it? Do you want some wine?"

He nodded. "Wine." He looked at Jo. "Heard…about… last night."

"How?" Jo asked.

"Doriana called," Lena said. "We had to come over to see how you and Franco are doing. We're sorry to barge in on you unannounced, but we were afraid if we called first, you'd tell us there was no need to stop over. And we wanted to see Franco for ourselves, to make sure he's okay. We're so glad Logan sent you to help him. At least he's not alone in this mess."

I'm glad I'm here too. The jarring thought popped into Jo's mind. "Let me get your wine," she said, channeling her thoughts elsewhere. "I need to stir the sauce and get the water boiling for the pasta."

Lena sniffed the air. "Smells wonderful. Is that my mother's recipe?"

"It might be. I found a container of sauce in the freezer."

"Franco's a good cook," Lena said.

Shocked, Jo choked, then hastily cleared her throat to cover it up. Franco a good cook? He did have a well-stocked kitchen. The guy was full of surprises, none of them like her impression of him all these years. She'd have to think about that some more.

Fifteen minutes later Jo's cell phone beeped, signaling a text message. Harris and Franco had arrived. She excused herself and ran to the door. She liked the older couple, but she'd never been good at small talk and fifteen minutes of it was more than she could handle. Through the peephole, she saw Harris open the passenger door, then Franco slide out and race up the steps. She disengaged the alarm and opened the door for him to slip through.

When he'd entered, she closed the door, then texted Harris. *Can U join us?*

Need 2 go home, he texted back.

She sighed. No Harris to act as her buffer between Franco and his parents.

She was in homemaker's hell. No, not really. Guilt for her uncharitable thought washed over Jo. She looked around the table. Lena and Dan were wonderful people who loved their kids and grandkids. But sitting at the dinner table with Franco and them and seeing the obvious love they felt for each other brought back her own tortured childhood. Watching Franco laugh at something Lena said filled Jo with bittersweet sorrow.

She'd never belonged anywhere. Some of her foster parents had been loving, but even in those homes she'd felt like the outsider she'd been her whole life. She poked at her salad. When her father had been alive, Jo had known her mother hadn't wanted her, but she'd had her dad, who'd adored her. He'd been with her for too short a time. And when he died... She wouldn't go there. She had a career she was good at, one that absorbed her, and that was all that mattered.

When dinner was over, Lena offered to help with the dishes, but Jo shooed Dan and her back into the living room. While Franco and she cleared the table, Jo finally had a chance to talk to him alone.

Setting dirty dishes on the kitchen counter, she turned as he came through the doorway balancing two dirty plates and two wine glasses in his hands. He'd taken a quick shower when he'd gotten home. Dressed now in jeans and a sweater, his hair slicked back, he looked so darn sexy, Jo wanted to devour him. The man managed to look hot in a kitchen surrounded by the remnants of their dinner. It wasn't fair.

He stopped when he saw her staring. "What?"

Pushing aside her sensual thoughts like a stack of dirty dishes, she locked gazes with him. "It's not safe for your parents to be here. It's not safe for anyone. You need to tell them they can't visit until the police find the people after you."

His jaw tightened. "I hate what those assholes trying to murder me are doing to my life."

Jo laid her hand on his forearm. His muscles flexed under her fingers. "Keep your voice down. You don't want your parents to hear. The police will catch the jerks who are after you, but you need to tell your parents to stay away for now."

Stepping back, he raked fingers through his hair. "I have a business to run, construction sites to visit, people depending on me."

"Suck it up, Callahan. You want to live, you'll listen to Harris and me." She put a hand on her hip. "You're still going to work, still maintaining your lifestyle, with a few restrictions."

Mouth tight, he stared at her. Then his shoulders relaxed and a look of resignation washed over his features.

"I'll tell my parents."

Half an hour later, they both walked Lena and Dan out to their Mercedes parked in front of Franco's house. While Franco and Lena helped Dan down the steps, Jo held back, gun at her side, nervously scanning the street. Traffic was light at this hour, but the people making Franco's life miserable could drive down the street any minute, guns blazing. Someone had already taken shots at him from a moving car.

When the couple drove away, Franco and Jo hurried back into the house, bolting the door behind them and resetting the alarm.

"I hate this so much," Franco said.

"I know. Things will get better. They'll get those jerks."

His mouth twisted in disgust. "The police have no leads. Not one."

"Not yet. Let's sit down. I need to pick your brain. With a little help from you, we can find the lead we're looking for. Are you up for it?"

He gestured for her to go ahead of him into the living room. "Ask all the questions you want, but I've told the police and you everything."

They settled onto the sectional and Jo turned to find Franco staring at her, a question in his eyes. "What?"

"I'm glad you're going shopping for some new clothes. With that face and that body, why do you hide behind those fatigues?"

She held up a hand. "Stop right there. This isn't about me or my clothes. This is about keeping you alive and helping the police find the guy or guys who are after you."

"What makes you think it's a guy?"

"What makes you think it's not? There's something you didn't tell the cops, isn't there? Someone you suspect?"

"No, there's not. It's just that you can't assume it's a man." He shrugged. "It's a guy calling me, but there could be a woman behind this. It's a thought."

She tapped her lip with her index finger. "I agree we have to keep all possibilities open. Whoever's trying to kill you has to be someone you know. Think, really think. Who could have it in for you? Any women out for revenge? Anyone with a fatal attraction to you?"

He laughed. "I like to think I'm too smart to go out with a woman like that."

"You and a bunch of other men."

He furrowed his brow. "I've broken up with women. Some of them…" He shrugged. "Most of them didn't want to let go."

"I always pegged you for a heartbreaker." She tried to keep her tone light, but a twinge of anxiety pulled at her. He'd shatter her heart too if she let him.

"I admit I've broken a few hearts, but the women knew from the beginning it wasn't going anyplace." He smiled and slid closer. "How many hearts have you broken, Ms. Josephine Fortune?"

She clenched a hand at her side, battling the old pain that his words provoked. "None, and we're talking about you. I'm not the one with some crazy person after me. So back off."

He sidled away. "Seriously, Jo, I can't imagine any of the women I dated trying to kill me." He furrowed his brow again. "I've given the police, you, and Harris the names of all the women I've dated in the past two years. There are no other names."

Jo grabbed her tablet she'd set on the coffee table earlier and powered it on. "I've got the names in here. I've already checked their Facebook pages, but couldn't find anything useful. I even did a spreadsheet with all their names, but nothing clicks. Let's go over each one. Maybe something will jog your memory, something that makes you think the woman might have it in for you. Okay?"

"If it is an old girlfriend with an ax to grind, why is she asking for money?"

Jo tapped the screen on her tablet. "Just go along with me. We have to consider every angle. The money thing could be to throw us off."

He nodded.

She went through the first five names, and Franco shook his head on each one. When she got to the sixth name, he hesitated.

"What?" She looked down at the screen again. "Lynn DiGiacomo. Is there something about her?"

"Could be. I didn't think it was important until now. I dated Lynn about eighteen months ago. We only went out for three weeks and we weren't exclusive with each other. I liked her, but she was clingy. After the first week, I couldn't take her constant phone calls and text messages demanding to know where I'd been and who I'd been with."

"How did you meet her?"

"You want a drink?" He stood and headed to the bar.

"I'll have water, but quit stonewalling."

"I'm not stonewalling. I'm thirsty." He opened the small refrigerator behind the bar and pulled out a bottle of beer and a bottle of water. He screwed off the caps on each and carried the bottles to the sectional, handing the water to Jo before sitting.

He took a long swig of his drink, then leveled his gaze at Jo.

"I met Lynn at one of the casinos in Atlantic City. She and I were guests at a birthday party for one of my clients. She was beautiful and I was attracted to her right away, but from the beginning she felt more for me." He shot Jo a self-deprecating grin. "At first, I liked having this extraordinarily beautiful and sexy woman crazy about me. But three weeks was all I could take of her insecurity and I stopped seeing her."

Jo took a swallow of her water and set her bottle down next to his on the table. "How did she take you cutting her loose?"

"Not well. She called me every day for a couple of weeks after that, always begging me to come see her or meet her somewhere. I finally realized she needed a friend, someone to talk to. We remained friends for about six months until she told me her husband was in prison."

Jo gasped. "She was married?"

He narrowed his eyes at her, then grabbed his beer and took another long swig. "I don't date married women. Despite my reputation, I have lines I won't cross and that's one of them."

"You didn't know she was married when you met her?"

"Of course not. Didn't you hear what I just said?"

Jo put her head back and released a deep sigh, then looked at him again. "You dated a woman whose husband was in jail? You broke her heart apparently. I'm sure dear hubby was glad to hear that."

"I wouldn't have thought she told him."

"Where's Lynn now? Where's the husband? And why didn't you tell the police?"

"You should be a cop with all these questions. Lynn's still in Rumson, New Jersey, far as I know. Her husband may have a different last name and I'm not sure if he's out of prison."

Jo entered the information into her tablet. "Why was her husband in prison?"

"Assault. It may have been mob-related. He apparently

did some work for them."

Jo groaned. "God save me." She held up a hand and counted off on her fingers. "You dated a woman whose husband was in prison. You broke her heart. Husband has mob ties. You didn't think to tell the police these little tidbits?"

"Lynn is a good person. I felt bad that I'd hurt her. She was always sad and needy. I couldn't risk hurting her again by bringing her into this. She'd cheated on her husband. I feel sure she didn't tell him about me, but if I told the police the whole story, they'd investigate her, and her husband might find out what she did. I couldn't do that to her."

"Aren't you the Sir Galahad?"

"Don't mock me, Jo. I know your impression of me, everyone's impression. Yeah, I've been wild and irresponsible, but there are things about me you don't know. No one knows. Believe it or not, I do have a heart."

Guilt pricked her conscience. She knew he had a good heart. She'd seen more and more of it lately. "I'm sorry, Franco. I shouldn't have said that. You didn't want her to get into trouble for cheating on her husband. I get that. But she knew full well what she was doing when she started the affair with you."

She held his gaze. "What am I going to do with you? You don't tell anyone about the kids and the cleaning lady who have keys to your house. You don't tell the police you dated a woman whose husband is in prison. A husband who has mob ties. I'm beginning to think you have a death wish."

CHAPTER EIGHT

Excitement surged through Jo. She bolted upright in her chair, rubbed her eyes, then stared back at the computer screen. Finally. Here was something—a possible lead in this case. She scrolled down the page and reread the police reports, making sure she hadn't missed anything. She pressed a hand to her thigh to stop the jittery movement her leg made whenever her instincts kicked in.

Salvatore DiGiacomo, husband of Franco's old flame Lynn DiGiacomo, had a sheet going back to his teen years. He'd recently served time for assaulting a man in a bar. According to the reports of eyewitnesses to the latest incident, DiGiacomo had tried to collect money the man owed him. When the guy couldn't pay and begged DiGiacomo for more time, DiGiacomo had refused and beat the guy badly enough to send him to the hospital for two weeks. DiGiacomo had been released from prison a month ago.

Jo's mind whirled with possible scenarios. She fist bumped the air.

Franco had said the guy might work for the mob. Could DiGiacomo have been trying to collect mob money from his victim? Sifting through her thoughts, she gazed off into the distance. The mob took retribution on its collectors who didn't do their jobs. DiGiacomo would know what the mob would do to him if he failed. If the victim hadn't come up with the money, DiGiacomo would still owe the mob. Knowing Franco was wealthy, maybe DiGiacomo was trying to shake him down for money to pay his debt. That way he could get revenge on Franco for sleeping with his wife and he'd get his money.

The fine hairs on her arms stood at attention as excitement swirled through her again. Yes, it could be. It was beginning to make sense.

Jo stretched her arms above her head and glanced at the microwave clock. Three a.m. Harris had promised to relieve her at four this morning so she could get some sleep before her shopping trip at ten. She rolled her eyes, blew out a breath, rubbed her lower back and twisted her head from side to side. Her stiff muscles protested her movements. The high stool she sat on didn't offer much support. She'd be achy all day, but spending the day doing criminal research held far more appeal than the torture of trying on clothes and shoes. Still, dressing the part of Franco's girlfriend was her job. And she always did her job.

Turning her attention back to the police reports, she reread the most disturbing part. No one knew where DiGiacomo was. She needed to call Logan, run some probables by him, get his sense, but with the time difference and her morning appointments, she'd have to wait. More time to clarify her thoughts then. She refocused on her computer screen.

One week after DiGiacomo's release he'd beaten his wife, Franco's ex-lover, leaving her with a broken arm and a broken nose. Then he'd disappeared, about the same time Franco's house had been ransacked. A warrant had been issued for his arrest on assault and parole violation.

Jo massaged her now-aching temples. After another thorough read-through, she wrote an email to Detective

Morelli citing her suspicions and requesting a picture of Di-Giacomo. None of the reports contained his picture. She hit "send" then sent an email to Logan and Harris telling them her findings, and that she'd call Logan later. She rubbed her hands together. She had a lead, a good one. They'd find Di-Giacomo and Franco would be safe.

Clothes, shoes, handbags, lingerie were strewn all over the bed and on the desk and chairs in the large guest bedroom. Sheesh. What was she going to do with all this stuff? The sight made Jo dizzy. Franco had been more than generous, giving her his credit card and free rein to buy whatever she'd wanted. Despite that, she'd tried to hold back, to be frugal. But Mitzi would have none of it. Acting like a fairy godmother on steroids, the older woman and the personal shopper at Neiman Marcus had dragged Jo into almost every department at the King of Prussia store.

Brewer had dropped her off forty-five minutes ago. Jo expected Franco back from work any minute.

A ping on her phone alerted her to a message. She grabbed her phone off the nightstand and looked down at the screen. Yes! A message from Detective Morelli thanking her for the information and promising to investigate the DiGiacomo lead immediately. He'd included a picture of Salvatore DiGiacomo. She narrowed her eyes at the screen. Her pulse spiked. This could be their perp. She studied the mug shot of the intimidating guy with the squiggly eyes and buzz cut. She wondered what his wife had seen in him. She had no doubts what the woman had seen in Franco. Most red-blooded women from eighteen to eighty would succumb to Franco's charms. *Even me.* Ignoring her wayward thoughts, she forwarded the picture to Logan and Harris.

A few minutes later, her phone rang. Harris. "Hey, man, are you here?"

"We're outside."

Jo raced down the stairs and disengaged the security alarm.

The front door opened and Franco slipped in. Although it was Saturday, Franco had put in a full day at work, and then some. At her insistence, his full security force had been in the building too. It was close to seven o'clock now. The fun-at-all-costs playboy she'd seen at family gatherings was nothing like the man she was coming to know.

"How was your shopping trip?" he asked, his intense gaze on her. Tension arced between them like an electrically charged summer storm.

"We got a lot of stuff."

"Let me see it." He smiled that wicked smile of his and leaned toward her until only a whisper separated them. He brushed back strands of her hair from her face. "I missed you."

The huskiness of his voice and the desire that gleamed from his eyes were almost her undoing. She swayed toward him, wanting to melt into the security and peace of his arms. The flash of triumph in his eyes shot her with a cold dose of reality and she stepped back, folding her arms across her chest as protection from her longings.

A mask seemed to slip over his face. The moment was lost. A twinge of regret settled in her chest.

She turned and walked up the stairs. He reset the alarm and followed her.

When they got to her room, he looked over to the bed where clothes covered the beige down comforter. "I see you had a good day."

"Mitzi and the store's personal shopper were more than helpful. I think they both got a vicarious thrill out of selecting all these clothes."

"I'm sure they did." He strode to the bed and began sorting through the garments, glancing at her and putting some to the side. Feeling suddenly disconcerted, she stood straighter, ignoring the hammering in her chest. Finally he picked up a green silk wrap dress with a low neckline. "This will look perfect on you. Get dressed. We go out in an hour."

"Wait a minute." She put a hand on her hip and glared at him. "Where do you get off ordering me around like that? You need to run your plans by me ahead of time, and I don't mean an hour before. I'll choose my own clothes. Where are you planning to go?"

He chuckled. "Jo, you are too much." Moving closer, he touched her chin with his fingers and tilted her head until their eyes met. "I don't mean to order you around. I'm used to issuing orders all day at work. Sometimes it's hard to shift gears. Please wear the dress. For me. It matches your eyes. We're going to a booksigning at a wine shop. I'd forgotten until my assistant reminded me about it today."

"A booksigning at a wine shop? You've got to be kidding."

"What better place to sign books? It's a surefire way to get a large crowd. The author is the wife of a big client and I have to go. Her book is a mystery set in a wine shop so the venue makes sense."

He bent and brushed his lips over hers. "Get dressed, beautiful. Harris will be here in an hour. You'll enjoy it. I promise."

<><><>

Harris pulled the car to the curb in front of the trendy

wine shop on Philadelphia's South Street. They sat in the car while Jo and Harris scanned the elegantly clad crowd waiting outside in an area roped off in red velvet, no less, to go into the shop. Curious onlookers stood on the other side of the ropes, gawking at the well-heeled people confined within the velvet.

Earlier the three of them had studied the picture of DiGiacomo. They'd be on the lookout for the suspect. "I don't like this," Jo said. "Too many people. DiGiacomo could be in this crowd. I thought this was invitation-only. Why are there so many bystanders?"

"Susan's book has been getting good reviews and she's making a name for herself among the locals," Franco said. "I guess people wanted to come out and see if they could get a glimpse of her." He smiled. "I suspect they also want a glimpse of the people privileged to get an invitation."

"I don't see anyone in that crowd who looks like DiGiacomo," Harris said. "I'm keeping the car here and I'll watch who comes and goes." He glanced toward the front of the shop. "Looks like they opened the doors. Wait until everyone's inside, then get out there." He turned in the driver's seat to look at Jo. "Keep your gun and your phone close. You'll both be safe."

Jo chewed her lip. "I'd feel better if we weren't here."

Agitation flashed over Franco's face. "This is an important client. I have to be here. I won't live like a hermit."

The frustration in Franco's voice ate at Jo like acid in her stomach. She hated living like this too. She blew out a breath. "I know, Franco. Let's get this show on the road. With Harris and me working together, nothing will happen to you."

Jo and Franco waited for Harris to open the passenger door. When Franco helped Jo from the car, the flash of cameras going off made her blink. As they walked toward the wine shop, she scanned the people milling around. Most looked merely curious. Certainly the invitees included some of the cream of Philadelphia society. With the cameras flashing, she felt like a celebrity on the red carpet. An unwelcome feeling.

Franco snaked his hand around her waist and pulled her closer to whisper in her ear. "I'm glad you wore that dress. You'll be the most beautiful woman here."

Pleasure heated her cheeks and warmed her insides. Then she reminded herself Franco was putting on a show for the photographers and others watching. The society gossips would be wagging tomorrow about playboy Franco Callahan's new woman. Their masquerade was working. Now if they could only flush out DiGiacomo before he got Franco. The thought sent chills skittering up her spine, cooling her pleasure at Franco's touch.

When they entered the shop, decorated like an elegant French villa, servers offered them something to drink. Franco took a flute of sparkling water with lemon and handed it to Jo before taking a glass of champagne for himself. Other servers walked around with trays offering a selection of appetizers—mushrooms stuffed with crab imperial, asparagus wrapped in prosciutto, crudités with dipping sauce, elegant cheeses with a wide variety of crackers.

The crush of the crowd forced Jo close against Franco. Her hip brushed his thigh as they maneuvered their way to the back of the store. The silk of her green dress swished around her bare legs. She knew the silver leather stiletto sandals made her legs look longer and emphasized her well-developed calves. A green crystal pendant on a silver chain hung between her breasts, shown to advantage by the low neck of the dress and the black lace push-up bra. She was unexpectedly aware of the feel of her silk thong between her thighs.

Franco tightened his arm around her waist as if he too had noticed the interested looks some of the men were giving her. Her new-found sexuality gave her a surprising feeling of power. She understood for the first time the control a sexy woman could wield over a man. A part of her liked it.

She reminded herself what she wore now was a uniform, no different from the fatigues she favored. But, silk and lace were worlds away from fatigues. The image of Franco lovingly undressing her, peeling the black silk thong down her legs, made erotic bliss flare deep inside her. She took a huge gulp of the water as if she could quench the liquid fire that raced through her veins.

When a waiter came by, she set her empty glass on his tray and waved away another drink.

"Enjoying yourself?" Franco asked, leaning toward her.

His unique scent of sandalwood teased her nostrils. "I'm fine." But she wasn't. She wanted him.

As they squeezed their way through the crowd, sampling some of the delicious tidbits of food, Jo constantly scanned the room, looking for anything unusual, perhaps someone who didn't look as if he or she belonged there.

Franco nodded to people they passed and stopped to talk to some. He always made sure to introduce Jo. The men were friendly, some openly assessing her with lust in their eyes. But the women barely acknowledged her. She could hear the cash registers going off in the women's heads as their hard eyes swept her, probably adding up the cost of her clothes and shoes. Determined to play her part, Jo gave each woman a smug smile. She was on the arm of one of Philadelphia's most notorious playboys and eligible bachelors. The way Franco held her close to his side, especially when he introduced her to other men, would convince the most hardened doubters that Franco and she were hot for each other.

She wasn't playing a part, a small voice whispered. She *was* hot for Franco. Very hot.

They finally reached the guest of honor, a plump middle-aged woman with sparkling blue eyes. Dressed in a conservative black dress, diamonds winked from her ears, throat and fingers. Jo glanced around. No one seemed to be paying any particular attention to them. She breathed a little easier.

"Franco, how wonderful to see you. Thanks for coming," the woman said when they stood in front of the table piled high with her books. She rose and leaned over to give him a peck on the cheek, then sat back down, still smiling. Her gaze went to Jo. While the other women had studied Jo with coldness, this woman's eyes were soft and friendly.

"Susan, congratulations on your book," Franco said. "I hear it's on its way to being a bestseller."

"From your lips to God's ears," she said with a self-deprecating laugh. "And who is this lovely young woman on your arm?"

"Susan Hoffman, Jo Fortune."

"I'm glad to meet you," Susan said. "Fortune. What an unusual name."

"It's French." Jo swallowed and clamped her mouth shut. She sounded like some unsophisticated country bumpkin. Despite her costly clothes, in this crowd she felt like domestic beer on a tray with a bottle of Dom Perignon. She drew herself up. "It's nice to meet you too," she added, giving the other woman a big smile. "Congratulations on your book."

"Thanks." Susan returned her smile, then turned to Franco. "I always knew the woman who would capture your heart was out there. I'm glad you found her. You two are a beautiful couple and anyone can see how in love you are."

Jo coughed. Franco patted her on the back.

A beaming Susan watched them. The woman thought she and Franco were in love. They were darn good actors.

For the next hour they mingled, stopping to talk to some of Franco's friends and acquaintances or perusing the wine shelves. Franco had purchased a book from Susan and handed it out to Harris who waited right outside the door. "No parking" signs adorned the street but the cops didn't bother Harris or the black Town Car parked at the curb. Money had its privileges, Jo thought. Also having a contact at the police department helped. Uniformed police were a visible presence outside to maintain crowd control. But Jo knew they were also keeping an eye out for DiGiacomo.

Although she never left Franco's side, she'd stayed alert, watching the guests and the servers. No one fit DiGiacomo's description. Jo began to relax as the evening wore on.

Finally it was time to leave. As they held hands and slipped out of the shop, Franco grabbed a handful of premium wrapped hard candies from a bowl by the door and stuffed them into his pocket. As he did, he looked at Jo and frowned.

"What's the matter?" she asked.

"Let's get in the car."

Harris held the car door for them and they slid in. Then he sank into the driver's seat and eased the car away from the curb.

Franco settled himself and reached into his pocket. "Harris, I grabbed a few pieces of that fancy candy for your sweet tooth. When I stuck them in my pocket, I felt something else." He pulled out a small piece of paper. "What's this? It's not mine." He turned on the overhead light and unfolded the paper. "Damn!"

"Let me see that," Jo said.

Without a word, he handed her the paper.

She held it by the edges and read.

I'm watching you was slashed across the paper in bold letters.

She raised her gaze to Franco's worried stare. "DiGiacomo wasn't in that crowd. I'm sure of it."

"Anyone could have brushed up against me and slipped that into my pocket," Franco said. "I knew most of the people there or knew of them. It could have been one of the servers."

Jo nodded. "Could be. Could also mean DiGiacomo isn't working alone. I'll call Morelli."

She leaned forward. "Harris, do you have something I can put this note in?"

"I always carry small plastic bags in the car just in case." He reached over and opened the glove compartment, pulled out a baggie and handed it to Jo. She carefully put the note in the bag and shoved the bag into her purse, then pulled out her phone to call the detective.

After Jo and Franco arrived at Franco's house, he locked the door and reset the security alarm, then followed her into the living room.

She sank into the leather sectional and set her purse on the table in front of her. The evening had been more fun than she'd expected, and there were times she'd forgotten she was working and let herself enjoy Franco's company. But that note in his pocket had disturbed her little oasis of peace.

"Drink?" he asked, holding up the crystal brandy decanter from the bar.

She shook her head. "You know I can't drink when I'm on duty."

"Want some water?"

"No. I'm good."

His gaze met hers from across the room. "Someday you won't be on duty." He grinned. "When that day comes, I'll take you out and get you drunk."

"As if." But she smiled. She suspected he wanted to dissolve some of the tension the note had engendered.

Carrying a brandy snifter half filled with amber cognac, he crossed the room and sat next to her. He held up his glass in salute. "To getting you drunk."

"Dream on."

He chuckled, then looked away while he sipped his drink. She studied his profile, his Italian heritage evident in his hawk-like nose and firm jaw. Despite his teasing, worry had glazed his eyes before he'd turned away.

Cradling his glass, he settled back in his seat. "What are your thoughts about this mess?"

"Some things don't make sense. If this was just a man out to hurt the guy who slept with his wife, he would have probably cornered you somewhere by now and beat the crap out of you."

Franco shot her a wry grin. "Thanks for the vote of confidence. You really think he could beat the crap out of me? I work out with a boxer once a week at the gym. And remember, I didn't know Lynn was married when we started our affair."

"I don't think our man DiGiacomo is going to cut you slack because of that. And don't believe for a minute that because you know a few boxing moves you can best a man like him in a street fight."

"Point taken."

"He's got someone helping him. He has to. Why would he hire people to help kill you? From what I've read about him, he could do that on his own. And why is he asking for money?" She widened her eyes as a thought forced its way into her mind. "Did Lynn give you money to hold for her?"

"I know what you're thinking. No, she didn't."

"I thought I was onto something, like maybe you were inadvertently holding mob money. There's something more going on here than we're seeing."

"No kidding. Don't worry your pretty little head about it now. It's late."

She bristled. "Don't patronize me."

"You're too easy, Josephine. I was teasing." He placed his glass on the table, then stood and reached down to take her hand and pull her up. "It is late."

They faced each other. He continued to hold her hand. She should pull free but she didn't want to. For just a little while, she'd enjoy the security of his nearness, of knowing somehow she wasn't alone. "I need to get out of these clothes," she finally said. "Then while you sleep I'll do some searches, see if I can come up with anything else on DiGiacomo."

"You work too hard." His eyes darkened. He released her hand and reached out to slide a finger along her low neckline. Delicious chills ran over her arms. "This dress looks unbelievable on you." He touched the pendant hanging in the shadow between her breasts, then his fingers followed, skimming the tops of her breasts exposed by the plunging neckline.

She bit back a groan. Her nipples puckered, and her breasts felt swollen, needy. "What are you doing?" she ground out.

"What does it feel like?" He caressed one breast, his thumb massaging the nipple through the silk and lace.

"We can't. I work for you."

"I know." Pulling her closer, he bent and lightly brushed his lips over her cleavage, then, with agonizing slowness, kissed his way to her neck.

She gripped his shoulders, fighting the fierce need his touch provoked. He continued to seduce her with hot kisses, his gentle caress of her breast. Her legs felt watery as if her bones were dissolving. With a low moan, she threw back her head, surrendering.

He kissed the sides of her mouth, then slid his tongue along the seam of her lips. He tasted like coffee and cognac as she opened to his invasion. Their tongues danced and mated in an erotic byplay.

Together, they slid onto the sectional, Franco on top of her. Hungry for him, Jo wrapped her arms around his neck and deepened the kiss. Her body on fire, she barely recognized her low moans of pleasure.

Finally, he pulled away and propped himself up on his elbows to stare down at her. "I want you."

The heat of his eyes held her captive. Words dried in her throat. She touched his face, his beautiful face. Her mind told her to stop. Her body craved him. Her soul needed him. What could it hurt to give into her needs just this once?

With a small smile, he slid off the sectional to kneel on

the floor next to her. Slowly, with tenderness, he slipped her dress off her shoulders to her waist, then he unclasped her bra and tossed it aside. His eyes, hot and wicked, seared her. "Delicious."

Cradling one of her breasts, he took the nipple into his mouth. Arching her hips, she scraped her fingers on the soft leather of the sofa and gave herself over to his skilled mouth and tongue.

He turned to her other breast, massaging, licking and sucking. A fresh wave of wetness seeped onto her lacy thong and hot need wracked her as Franco continued his exquisite torture. Something began to build in her, a raging storm she couldn't control. Nothing existed but her and Franco and the desperate need that slammed the breath out of her. Little cries broke from her as she twisted beneath him.

"Not yet, Jo."

Did she imagine the slight tremble in his voice?

He straightened and slipped a hand under her dress, stroking the inside of her thigh. Burning desire overtook her. Moaning, she gave herself over to his sensual touch. He pushed her dress up to her waist, then slid off her thong. Exposed now to the desire that flamed from his eyes, she gasped and put out a hand to shield her most private parts from his gaze.

Gently brushing her hand away, he said, "Easy. I won't hurt you." He stroked the curls at the apex of her thighs.

She bit her lip as old memories, old fears pressed against her mind. No, she wouldn't let the memories in. She wanted Franco. He wasn't like the others. He wouldn't hurt her. She trusted him.

Then he was kissing her there, so tenderly, so not like those other times. She began to relax, to surrender. When he

CARA MARSI

slipped one finger, then another into her, she almost purred. He moved slowly at first, then faster and harder.

She gripped the edge of the cushion and twisted her head from side to side as her whimpers of pleasure filled the room.

"Like that?" he rasped.

"Yes," she croaked out.

Need, molten and overwhelming, built in her, a tempest growing stronger and stronger. The storm rolled over her in flaming waves, taking her to a place she'd never been. All thought fled as he drove his fingers into her. Heat pumped into her veins and an ache built between her legs. Her world spun out of control. She cried out his name as shudders racked her.

When her trembling body settled down, Franco slid his fingers out of her and kissed her mound. Then he brushed the hair from her face. "Okay?"

She opened her eyes to his scorching gaze. "More than okay. That was...wonderful. I've never...that's never..."

He furrowed his brow. "You've never...what, Jo?"

Embarrassment warmed her cheeks. "I've never..." She took a deep breath. "I've never felt like that before. That's never happened."

With gentleness, he fixed her dress to cover her nakedness, then helped her sit. He sat next to her and gathered her to him, stroking her hair. "You've never had an orgasm before?"

She buried her face in his neck and shook her head. He was a man of the world, he'd been with sophisticated women. What must he think of her?

"You haven't been with the right man, Jo."

The right man. His words hit her with the force of a pail

of cold water thrown in her face. She couldn't tell him those things she'd kept hidden. She didn't want his pity, or worse, his disgust. When she'd confessed her darkest secret to her ex-fiancé, he'd thrown her aside in revulsion. She couldn't handle Franco's rejection.

She pushed against him and stood. He stood with her, a confused look on his face. When he reached for her, she flinched and stepped away, putting the coffee table between them.

"What's wrong?" he asked.

"That was wrong. All wrong."

"It was right. Very right." He moved to the other side of the table and leaned close. "You want me as much as I want you," he said with quiet determination. "I'll get past whatever armor you've got. And when I do, I'll make you mine."

Anger flared. She pulled it around her like a heavy coat. "You don't own me. No one does, especially not some man." She blinked away tears, hiding her fears. "Don't touch me again, Franco."

"You don't mean that."

"Try me." Even as she said the words, she knew it was an empty threat. Franco Callahan could melt her with a touch or a look. She'd have to be careful

Because she knew Franco didn't really want her. He wanted the conquest.

CHAPTER NINE

Monday afternoon, loud cursing, followed by the rattle of a key being forced into a lock had Jo instantly awake and alert. She jumped out of bed, grabbed her jeans and a T-shirt from the chair and yanked them on. A quick glance at the bedside clock told her it was just before two in the afternoon. Still adjusting her top, she scooped up her gun and raced down the stairs.

Voices came from the other side of the front door, then the rattling sound of a key again. Good thing she'd convinced Franco to change the locks. Apparently whoever was out there had a key to the old lock. She sighed. Still another individual Franco had given a key to?

She looked through the peephole. Three teens, two Hispanic-looking and one African-American, huddled together, staring at the door and cursing.

"What do you want?" she shouted through the door.

All three heads jerked up and looked around.

Finally one of the Hispanic youths said, "We came to water Mr. Franco's plants and take out the garbage."

"He told you he didn't need you for awhile."

"We came anyway," the black youth said. "He's payin' us to do nothin'. We're no slackers. We work for our money."

"For God's sake," Jo muttered. Her sleep was interrupted for this? "What are your names?"

The African-American kid stepped away from the door so she could see him more easily. He touched his chest. "I'm Marcus." Tilting his head, he said, "And this here is Pedro and this is Felipe."

The others stepped back too and nodded.

"Just a minute," she said.

Somehow she believed the kids. But in her line of work she'd learned to take no one at face value. Without a tangible lead as to who was after Franco, she'd take no chances. Hurrying into the living room, she snatched up the phone and punched in Franco's cell phone number.

He answered immediately. "What's wrong?"

"There are three young men standing at your door, wanting to come in and water your plants and take out the garbage. Their names are Marcus, Pedro, and Felipe. Sound like anyone you know?"

"What are they doing there? I told them to stay away."

"Apparently you didn't make yourself clear."

"They're okay. Let 'em in."

"All right, I will and I'll also make sure they understand they can't come back." She disconnected the call and hoped these were the last of her unexpected visitors.

Jo disengaged the security alarm, and holding her gun behind her back, cautiously opened the door. A quick look showed no one else on the street.

"Get in here." She stood aside to usher them in, then closed the door and locked it.

Giving her astonished looks, they crowded into the entry way. They were all scrawny as hell. She could take them down easily if necessary.

"Who are you?" Pedro asked.

"I'm a friend of Fra...Mr. Franco's."

They gave her assessing looks, as if they couldn't quite believe Franco had a woman living there, or maybe they knew his reputation with leggy blondes. She didn't fit the stereotype, especially with her hair mussed and wearing jeans and a T-shirt, and with her feet bare and her hand behind her back.

"What's your name?" Marcus asked.

"Jo."

"Funny name for a girl," Felipe said.

"Can we go into the living room?" Pedro asked.

"Go ahead." Before following them, she engaged her gun's safety, then shoved the gun behind her into the waistband of her jeans and pulled her T-shirt over it.

"Mr. Franco asked you not to come for awhile," she said after they'd all edged into the living room.

Felipe's brown eyes studied her. He seemed to decide she was okay because he visibly relaxed. "We know, but it ain't right he pays us for not working. He taught us to give a good day's work for pay. "

"What do you mean, Mr. Franco taught you?" Jo asked.

"He teaches us things, at the center," Marcus said.

"He owns the center," Pedro said.

"No he doesn't, you jerk," Felipe said. "The city owns it."

"He pays for it, and you're a jerk," Pedro said with narrowed eyes.

"Boys, that's enough," Jo said. "What center is this?"

"The Second Chance Youth Center in North Philly," Marcus said.

"And Franco comes there a lot?" she asked.

Felipe shook his head. "Not so much anymore, but he

said he'd be back. Is he in trouble?"

"No," Jo lied. She didn't want to drag them into this mess. She also had to be sure they didn't come back until the police caught whoever was after Franco. She'd never forgive herself if anything happened to these kids.

She glanced at the wall clock, then back at Marcus. "It's only two o'clock. Shouldn't you all be in school?"

"Nah," he said. "No school today. It's a teacher service day or somethin'."

"Okay then. You guys do what Mr. Franco's paying you to do. I have some fresh-made iced tea in the refrigerator. How about some of that when you're done?"

"Cool," Pedro said.

Smiling, Jo moved closer to them, hopefully gaining their trust. "Listen up, guys. I know you want to help Mr. Franco, but you really can't come back here until he tells you it's okay. What if I make sure he gives you lots of extra work later so you know you've earned your salaries? What do you think?"

"Um," Marcus said, looking at the ceiling.

"Okay with me," Felipe said.

"Me too," from Pedro.

"I guess," Marcus said.

"Cool, guys. Now get to work and I'll get that tea ready."

What had they meant about the youth center? There was a whole side of Franco Callahan she knew nothing about.

◇◇◇

Jo stifled a yawn and sipped more of her coffee, her fourth cup of the day. She hadn't been able to get back to sleep after the kids left. They'd worked hard, taking their tasks seriously. She smiled. If Franco had instilled that work

89

ethic in them, he'd done a good job.

As she sat at the kitchen island, the quiet closed around her, a silent reminder of the loneliness of her life, especially now, all by herself in Franco's expensive townhome. She'd liked having the three boys here, hearing their laughter as they teased each other. She'd been sorry to see them go.

Franco would be home soon, then her loneliness would be shoved aside for a time. She ran her hand over the rim of her mug as desire, unwanted and unbidden, stole over her. Whenever Franco was near, everything around her, even the most mundane objects, seemed to take on a new vibrancy. He brought excitement and a lust for life that encompassed all he touched, even her.

She closed her eyes and let the memory of his love-making two nights ago roll through her mind, imagining his hands and mouth on her again. Her dreams had been filled with erotic images of him, disrupting her sleep. She pressed a hand to her stomach, reliving the wildness and passion he'd incited. And the climax that had sent her to the stars and back. Could he do it again? Would he try? He'd left her to herself since that tumultuous evening after the wine shop booksigning, apparently backing down from the challenge she'd flung at him to "try her."

Yesterday, Sunday, Harris had driven Franco to the gym early. When he got home, he'd closeted himself in his home office. Other than eating takeout together, they'd managed to avoid each other. But today she had to face him.

Her cell phone rang and she jumped, grateful for the noisy intrusion. She snatched the phone off the counter and looked at the name on the ID, then grinned.

"Hey," she said. "Are you on your way?"

"Hey, darlin', we're headin' out now," Harris said.

"You need anything?"

"No, I'm good."

"See you in fifteen."

"Thanks, man."

A little more than fifteen minutes later she heard the sedan pull up and ran to look through the peephole, then opened the door to Franco. Watching him race up the steps, that sculpted body the well-cut gray suit couldn't quite hide, the short dark hair and the brilliant blue eyes, revived her long-abandoned wish for a home and family. Husband, kids, dog, cat, the works.

He winked at her as he slid through the door, and once again she remembered what they'd done the other night. Her face burned hotter than the desert on a scorching day.

She waved to Harris, then closed the door, locked it, and reset the alarm. When she turned around, Franco was staring at her.

"What?" Her hand instinctively shot up to wipe her mouth. "Do I have food on my face?"

He smiled that lopsided smile of his, and her heart did a little flip.

"You're so damn sexy," he said.

She pressed against the door. "Let's not go there. We need to talk, mister. Like, right now."

He loosened his tie. "I need to get out of these clothes. How about you pour me a glass of wine and we'll talk as soon as I change. That Pinot Noir I opened the other night will do."

"Do I look like your maid?"

He stepped closer. "Please pour me a glass of wine, Jo," he said, speaking soft and low. "If you will."

She slid away from the unwanted note of intimacy in

his voice. "Get changed and meet me in the kitchen."

"Sure thing, boss." With a salute, he bounded up the stairs.

She couldn't help smiling as she headed toward the wine rack.

Jo set his filled wine glass at one end of the center island. The woodsy aroma of the wine teased her nostrils and tempted her. Once this assignment was over, she'd drink a whole bottle of Pinot Noir. With a last, longing look at the deep burgundy liquor, she settled onto a seat at the other end of the counter, her tablet in front of her.

"Hey," he said, coming into the kitchen. He glanced at her tablet. "This looks serious."

Dressed in a dark blue T-shirt and tight-fitting faded jeans, Franco was smokin' hot. She only had so much willpower.

"Sit," she said. "I need answers and you're going to give them."

Eyebrows raised, he straddled one of the stools and picked up his wine. He took a sip, set the glass down on the granite top and caught her gaze. "This has something to do with the guys who were here today, doesn't it?"

She nodded. "It's not safe for them to be here. What if whoever's after you had gotten hold of the boys? I thought you were going to make it clear they can't come here for awhile."

He held up his hands. "I did. I had no idea they'd show up."

"I don't think they'll be back until you tell them it's okay. I worked out something with them. When they do come back, you need to give them lots of work. Apparently you've instilled a real work ethic in them, and you need to make them feel they're earning what you pay them."

"Lady, with that tone of voice you could run some of my construction sites. You'd straighten those guys right out."

The teasing gleam in his eyes broke her resolve and made her smile.

"You're even more beautiful when you smile," he said. "You should do that more often."

Trying to cover her discomfort at his compliment, she picked up her tablet. Feeling more in control, she raised her gaze to his. "I think you haven't been completely honest with us, Franco. We need to know everything about your life if you expect us to protect you and the police to catch the people after you."

His eyes hardened to blue chips, the teasing light gone. "I've told you and the police everything I think you need to know. There are parts of my life that are private, and they'll stay that way."

Hurt knotted into a tight ball in her chest. Two nights ago she'd trusted him with her body, but he wouldn't trust her when his life might depend on it.

Jo set her tablet on the counter, pressed her palms on the cool granite, and leaned toward him. "That's the problem. You aren't allowed to keep parts of your life secret. Don't you get that?"

"I get it, but I don't like it."

"Too bad. You're not making the decisions here. I am." She sighed, settled back and picked up the tablet again. "The boys talked about a youth center. Tell me about it. And I want the truth."

"Okay, okay." He blew out a breath and raked fingers through his hair as though he were about to argue and thought better of it. "About ten years ago I helped start a center for disadvantaged kids in the inner city. We've done good work, getting the kids off the streets, teaching them skills. During the summer I hire some of the older ones to work at my company's construction sites. The center has great volunteers. We try to teach the kids to handle money and take personal responsibility. The kids who were here today are three I'm mentoring. They're good kids."

Stunned, Jo put down her tablet. "You've done all that? You have a good heart, Franco Callahan."

He shot her a self-deprecating smile and picked up his wine glass, studying the red liquid. "Don't tell anyone. It would ruin my reputation." He sipped his drink, not looking at her. When his gaze met hers again, hurt flashed in his eyes. "No one will believe you anyway."

"I believe you."

"Really? Jo Fortune thinks I have a heart? Now I know I'm slipping."

She rolled her eyes, then picked up her tablet again. "Tell me about the center. Why did you start it? Who helped you?"

"I'm hungry," he said, setting down his glass. He got up and strode toward the huge side-by-side refrigerator. "Do you want a sandwich?"

With a frustrated sigh she shoved her tablet aside. Getting anything out of Franco was harder than cracking a titanium double-lock safe. "Okay. I'll help." She started to get up, but he waved her back down.

"Stay comfortable. I don't need help. I make a mean sandwich."

She lowered herself onto the stool and watched as he pulled rolls, a piece of leftover chicken breast, tomatoes, lettuce, cheese, an avocado and condiments from the refrigerator. Opening a cabinet door, he took out two plates.

Without looking at her, he finally said, "I got into some trouble when I was a kid. Little stuff, stuff my dad was always able to smooth away. But then I did something really stupid. When I was seventeen, I stole a car."

"You're kidding."

He glanced her way. "Pretty bad, huh?" With a shrug he went back to assembling the sandwiches. "I avoided juvie, but I had to give a year of community service. I was only too glad to do anything the court asked to stay out of that hellhole."

Jo put a hand to her mouth, wondering what he'd say if he knew she'd barely escaped juvie herself.

"I did my community service at a youth center, teaching the kids reading, writing, helping with some sports," he continued. "I saw a side of this city and a side of life I didn't know existed. All through college I kept thinking about the kids I'd met at that center." He put down the knife he was using to slice the chicken and turned to her. "Some of those kids lived lives of total desperation with no hope of anything good ever happening. I had to do what little part I could to make things better." He picked up his knife again and went back to slicing. "Whatever I do is never quite enough though. But I won't ever stop."

She knew what he meant on a level most people didn't. Would that surprise him? Probably. At the regret in his voice, she pushed up from her stool and went to him. He turned to look at her.

"I know, Franco," she said. "We all do the best we can with what we're given. There are some things that are out of our control." A small voice urged her to tell him more, to share her own soiled past. But she couldn't.

The knife fell out of his hand onto the counter with a clang. Franco gathered Jo into his embrace and held her tight.

"We can't solve all the problems of the world." Her voice was muffled.

He pulled away and held her at arm's length, his hot blue gaze studying her. He kissed her lightly on the lips. "We're not going to solve any of the problems of the world— tonight at least. Let's eat."

Later, Jo pushed away her empty plate. "That was good. You were right. You do make a mean sandwich."

"Thank you, ma'am. I aim to please."

His teasing grin reminded her he knew how to please her in so many ways. The thought pushed into her mind like a spring bud reaching toward the light, soft and filled with promise. Trying to cool her rising libido, she reached for her tablet, one of the tools of her trade, and tonight a weapon against her traitorous body and mind.

"I have more questions." As they'd eaten, they'd made small talk, but she had to get back to business.

He shifted on his stool and smiled. "I figured you weren't through with me."

She ignored his double-entendre and the mischievous glint in his eyes. "You started the center ten years ago. That would be when you were twenty-five. Why haven't I heard of this before?"

"Because no one in my family knows."

"You've got to be kidding. How could they not?"

"I didn't want them to know. I got a nice chunk of money from my parents when I graduated from college and I invested that. I'm a silent partner in the center and that's the way I like it."

"Who's the other partner?"

He blinked and looked away.

"Franco?"

When he turned back to her, a look of resignation washed over his features. "My original partner was Bob MacIntyre. Mac. He'd been my best friend since high school. We started the center and the charitable group to fund it. Mac was chief financial officer."

"What happened?"

"He died."

"How?"

His features closed. "He died in prison. And that's all I'm going to say."

Her instincts told her there was a lot more to this story, that Mac's death affected Franco more than he wanted to admit. She resolved to get more out of him later.

"I've answered your questions," he said. "Now I have some of my own."

"I don't have to answer your questions. You're the one in trouble."

"Who hurt you?"

Anxiety and shame pressed into her chest, stifling her breath. She tried to look away, but the concern in his eyes drew her like a moth to flame.

"Tell me, Jo."

She didn't know what to say. What to do. How could he have guessed?

She blinked back tears. "I'll clean up. You go relax."

CHAPTER TEN

Jo looked both ways instinctively, though it was a one-way street. Franco was already safe inside the car. After she slid into the back seat, Harris closed her door and sank his heavy bulk into the driver's seat. He popped a piece of hard candy into his mouth before pulling away from the curb. The butter-soft leather upholstery whispered around her as she settled in. She stole a glance at Franco, careful to keep distance between them. With his dark indigo jeans, white T-shirt and black leather jacket, his short hair slightly mussed, and a day's growth of dark stubble, his dangerous, sexy appeal made her heart hammer and her mind conjure erotic fantasies. It had been a whole week since he'd given her that mind-blowing orgasm.

Get over it already. He has.

He hadn't touched her in a sexual way since that night.

The car purred along, headed toward I-95 and the New Jersey Turnpike to Rumson, where Lynn DiGiacomo lived. Jo could think of better ways to spend an April Saturday than visiting one of Franco's former girlfriends.

She absently brushed a hand along her denim-covered thigh. The designer jeans were shockingly expensive, as were her yellow combed cotton sweater and glove-soft tan leather jacket. Her mid-heel boots were the same leather as the jacket. She hated to admit it, but the well-fitting jeans that hugged her butt and the leather boots and jacket, so different from the loose-fitting androgynous fatigues she favored, made her feel special and feminine. She was getting used to being a woman, to showing off her figure. Appalled at the direction of her thoughts, she sucked in a breath and concentrated on watching the city flash past as the smooth-riding car ate up the roadway.

"You really think this is going to work?" Franco asked, drawing her attention.

She faced him, grateful to talk business. "Your girlfriend won't talk to the police but she agreed to see you. If she's telling the truth that she's got information that might help us, it's worth a shot."

A muscle twitched in his jaw and his brow furrowed. "She was never my girlfriend. We only dated a few weeks. I don't quite trust Lynn. She doesn't always tell the truth. She likes to please. She used to do whatever I asked and she'd tell me whatever she thought I wanted to hear." His eyes met Jo's. "I like my women with a little fight in them. And a lot of honesty."

"Could have fooled me. I thought you liked shallow, malleable women."

"I dated women like that because they expected nothing from me but a good time. No one ever expected much from me anyway so why not enjoy myself?"

"Sure, why not? *Carpe diem* and all that." Despite her glib reply, she'd seen the way his eyes shadowed. She forced herself to look out the window again. The intimate confines of the car were playing havoc with her emotions. For a second, she'd thought Franco had allowed her a glimpse into his soul. How foolish.

As if realizing he'd revealed too much, his voice took

on that arrogant note she knew so well. "Jealous, Jo? Maybe those women have, or had, something you want."

She twisted her head around to face him. "You're disgusting."

"Losing your cool, Ms. Fortune? I must be getting to you."

Refusing to answer, she turned toward the window again. Franco was getting to her all right. Pieces of her hard-won control, along with pieces of her heart, crumbled a little more every day she spent with him. She should have fought Logan harder when he presented her with this assignment.

To Jo's relief they spent most of the rest of the two-hour trip strategizing their meeting with Lynn DiGiacomo and going over everything that had happened to Franco, trying to tie the pieces together. It had been Jo's idea to visit Lynn when Detective Morelli reported the woman had refused to speak to the police. When Franco had called Lynn, she'd readily agreed to his visit, promising she had useful information about her husband. Jo had felt a twinge of jealousy at the way the other woman jumped at the chance to see Franco again.

No surprises there. She knew exactly why his ex-girlfriends still wanted him.

Franco directed Harris through Rumson. They passed elegant McMansions, each one seemingly larger than the one before it. Finally they stopped at a gated driveway. Harris pressed the call button to announce them. When the gate swung open, they headed down the winding drive.

The drive ended in a flower-filled circle before a large, tan stucco house. White columns fronted the house which had a wraparound porch. An enclosed sunroom jutted from one side of the structure. A detached five-car garage was visible on the other side.

"Holy Tony Soprano," Jo said. "I swear I've seen this house on TV."

"Maybe the wealthy housewives of wherever?" Franco said.

"Seriously? She was on TV?"

He laughed. "No, but Lynn is a former model. She could definitely be one of the housewives."

"Or a mob wife."

"That too."

Harris pulled to a stop, then opened the back door for Jo and Franco.

"I'll wait here," Harris said, glancing around. "Looks clear so far. Ms. DiGiacomo said she has security cameras around the property and a security detail so we should be okay."

Franco placed a hand on the small of Jo's back. "Shall we?"

She adjusted her designer bag. It hit against the small shoulder holster she'd elected to wear today under her jacket. They headed up the tan brick walkway to the wide brick steps. The steps led to the porch and the ornately carved double oak doors flanked by stained glass windows.

Franco reached up to ring the bell, but before his finger touched the button, the door flew open.

A statuesque blonde, who would have been stunning except for the yellowish bruises under her eyes, the bandage partially covering a swollen nose, and her arm in a sling, stood at the opened door and smiled at Franco. Her injuries couldn't hide the perfect white teeth and the clear green eyes that softened as she looked at him. A low-cut white sweater barely contained the most magnificent breasts Jo had ever seen. Probably man-made.

"Franco," the woman breathed in a smoky voice. "I've missed you." Ignoring Jo, she ran her hand down his arm, as if she needed to reassure herself he was real. "Come in." She slid aside to let them into a black and white marble-floored entryway. The heavy scent of the woman's perfume made Jo cough as she slipped past. Even in her heels, Jo only came up to the woman's shoulders.

A hulking man, a weightlifter by the size of the biceps bulging from the short sleeves of his black T-shirt and the massive thighs outlined by the tight jeans, stood inside the doorway, studying them. His short dark hair shouted Special-Ops. No doubt one of Lynn DiGiacomo's security detail.

As Jo preceded Franco through the door, her gaze swept upward. A crystal chandelier hung from a high ceiling that soared two floors. A winding staircase led to a landing dominated by a stained glass window with a picture of a tall blonde, naked and riding a white horse. The blonde was a dead ringer for Lynn. The oddly disturbing image made a chill skitter over Jo.

She lowered her gaze to take in the entry hall. Gilded statues lined walls covered in gold brocade. Jo had seen many elegant homes in her line of work, but none quite so gaudy as this.

"Lynn, this is Jo," she heard Franco say.

She looked at Lynn and smiled, ready to put on a polite mask.

The blonde's green eyes, so soft when she looked at Franco, hardened as she scrutinized Jo.

"A pleasure, I'm sure." Lynn raised one exquisitely arched eyebrow. Disdain on her face, she looked Jo up and down. Seeming to dismiss Jo, the woman turned to Franco with a dazzling smile. "Let's go into the living room."

Franco took Jo's hand as they followed Lynn into the large room to the right of the entryway. Jo had to hand it to the other woman. Wearing skintight jeans and six-inch heels that clicked on the marble floor, Lynn's movements were fluid, graceful, and suggestive. Four-inch heels Jo could handle, but she knew if she wore those pants with those sky-high heels on that floor, she'd be down on her butt.

French doors, open to a large flagstone-paved patio, took up one wall of the cavernous living room, done in black, white and red. A black baby grand piano stood in one corner. Couches and chairs in shades of red were scattered around the room. Marble-topped tables in varying sizes nestled among the chairs and sofas. Lynn gestured to an overstuffed couch done in red velvet. Jo and Franco settled in while Lynn sat opposite in a matching chair.

Lynn's bodyguard followed them and went to stand behind her. He rested a proprietary hand on Lynn's shoulder. She twisted around to look up at him and pat his hand before turning her attention back to Jo and Franco.

"This is Tim Sheehan, one of my bodyguards," Lynn said.

Jo and Franco nodded at the bodyguard. He gave them a curt nod in return, his hard gray eyes challenging, as if daring them to make a move to hurt Lynn. Franco had said Lynn was insecure. Some people never learned. Would Lynn's husband come after Sheehan once he was done with Franco?

"Would you like something to drink?" Lynn asked.

"Thanks, but I'm good," Franco said. "We had a light lunch in the car on the way up." He looked at Jo. "How about you?"

"I'm good." She fidgeted. Even if she were starving

she wouldn't say so. Uncomfortable in the gaudy surroundings and facing one of Franco's ex-lovers, she wanted out of there as quickly as possible.

Through the years, she'd seen Franco with other women and it had never bothered her this much. Refusing to acknowledge why the thought of him making love to other women affected her now, she refocused on her job and the reason they'd come all this way.

Lynn settled back in her chair, wincing a little as she touched her injured arm. "I was surprised and happy to hear from you, Franco."

He leaned forward. "Lynn, I'm sorry for what happened to you. If I'd known you were in danger from your husband—"

She waved a hand, cutting him off. "You couldn't have known, and I knew exactly what I was getting into when we started our affair. Sal's beat me before this, and I've no doubt he'll try again." She turned around to smile at Sheehan, then looked back at them. "That's why I have Tim and the rest of my security detail. I don't go anywhere alone nowadays."

"That's no way to live," Franco said. "I know. I've had a taste of that myself. The police told you we think your husband may be the one trying to kill me."

Sadness darkened Lynn's eyes as she nodded. "I'm not surprised. He threatened to go after you when he was through with me. He would have killed me this last time if I hadn't run out of the house. The gardener saw us and called the cops." Tears glistened in her eyes and she clasped her hands together on her lap. "I didn't tell him about us, Franco. I swear. He put a tail on me when he was in prison. I didn't know. I'm sorry."

Jo stiffened. "You knew your husband would come after Franco, but you didn't tell the police?"

Franco put his hand on Jo's thigh and squeezed gently as Lynn's mouth set in a grim line. "Sal beat the shit out of me. I was afraid if I told the cops about him going after Franco, he'd come back here and finish the job. I was scared, Franco. Please believe that."

"I understand," Franco said in a soothing voice. Jo guessed he was trying to gain Lynn's trust so she'd tell them anything that might help them locate her husband. Jo gripped the seat cushions, fighting for patience when what she really wanted to do was shake the information out of the woman.

Lynn turned to Jo with narrowed eyes. "You the new girlfriend?"

Jo nodded. She and Franco had decided they'd keep up the pretense with Lynn on the chance she was still in touch with her husband. They didn't want him tipped off that Franco had round-the-clock protection.

"You sure don't look like Franco's type," Lynn said.

"This isn't about my girlfriends." Franco's sharp voice cut into the tense atmosphere. "We have to find your husband. You said you could help us."

Lynn chewed her lip. "I don't know where Sal is. I haven't seen him since the night he did this to me." Blowing out a breath, she glanced toward the French doors.

Beside Jo, Franco tensed. "What the hell?" he said, his voice harsh. "We came all the way up here because you said you had information that would help us find him, information you couldn't give the police."

Lynn shifted a furtive gaze to Franco. "Maybe I just wanted to see you again." Despite her flirty words, fear flashed from her eyes. "Sal's got friends and contacts all over New Jersey and Pennsylvania. He could be anywhere."

Her voice trembled slightly and she lowered her eyes. Jo's instincts went on alert. Lynn was hiding something.

"Let's settle down and see what you do know," Jo said, hoping her falsely calm voice would put Lynn at ease and encourage her to talk. "Does he still drive a black Cadillac Escalade?" Jo had tapped into the New Jersey and Pennsylvania DMV records. The Escalade, with New Jersey plates, was the only car registered to Salvatore DiGiacomo. And someone in a black Escalade had taken shots at Franco.

Frowning, Lynn looked at Jo. "How do you know that? You a cop?"

Franco took Jo's hand in his and squeezed. "We got the information from the Philly police. Jo is worried about me. That's all." Still holding Jo's hand, he moved to the edge of his seat. "Lynn, tell us what you know. Don't you want your husband put away so he can't hurt anyone again?"

She chewed her lip. "Yeah, I do, but I'm afraid. It's why I didn't tell the police."

"What has you too scared to tell the police?" Franco asked.

"Because of who's involved. If they find out I talked to the police, I'm dead. I'll tell you, but don't tell the cops it came from me." She leaned forward, a conspiratorial look on her face. "I think Sal's with his latest girlfriend. Her uncle is high up in the Philly mob. Sal has some mob ties, but he's strictly small potatoes. If I bring the cops down on the niece, I'll pay."

Jo straightened. She'd never understand some people. "Your husband has a girlfriend?"

Lynn barked a bitter laugh. "Sal always has a girlfriend or two. Yet he beats the shit out of me every time I fool around."

Jo pulled her hand from Franco's. "You've had other lovers since you've been married?"

"Yeah. So what of it? How many married people do you know who don't fool around?"

Jo thought of Logan and Doriana. "I know a few." She met Lynn's gaze. "Has your husband tried to kill any of your lovers before?"

"No."

"Then why is he going after me?" Franco asked.

Lynn's eyes softened as she looked at Franco. "Because you're the only one I've ever fallen in love with. The only one I'm still in love with."

Jo shot a glance at Lynn's new lover standing behind her. The other man's face remained impassive. Jo guessed he didn't care much if Lynn had feelings for another man. She almost felt sorry for the other woman. Unless she got help, she'd only keep making the same mistakes over and over again.

Franco's thigh brushed Jo's as he shifted and cleared his throat. "Do you know where this girlfriend lives?"

Jo wondered if Franco felt as uncomfortable as she did.

Lynn nodded. "South Philly."

"Can you give us the address?" Franco asked.

"I'll write it down." Lynn went to a small desk partially hidden in a corner and opened a drawer, pulling out a sheet of paper and a pen. She hastily wrote something, then strode to Franco and handed him the paper.

He glanced at it, then looked up at Lynn. "Thanks. I'll give this to the police. Anything else you can think of?"

A stricken look came into Lynn's eyes. "Please keep me out of it."

"We will."

"Lynn," Jo said, getting the other woman's attention. "The person or persons after Franco keep telling him they want the money. We don't know what money they're talking about. Do you know anything about that? Is Sal broke? Why would he ask for money?"

Lynn sat back in her chair, her body tense. "I can't imagine why he'd ask for money. Look around you. Does this look like we're broke?"

"No," Jo said. "But seeing isn't always believing."

"Are you sure about the money?" Franco asked. "Your husband could be belly up and doesn't want to tell you. Or he could have gambling debts, or owe the mob."

Lynn shrugged. "Sal drops loads in Atlantic City and Vegas, but far as I know, he's always paid his debts. And he knows better than to owe the mob. Although." She stopped, then shook her head. "No. I can't see him asking you for money."

Franco took Jo's hand again and squeezed. "Whoever is after me threatened Jo. Would your husband threaten her? And why?"

Lynn let out another short, brittle laugh. "That's easy. Tit for tat. You took me so he's gonna take something of yours."

"Anything else, Lynn?" Franco asked. "Anything at all you think might help?"

"Nope. Nothing."

"You have my number. Call me if you think of anything. And we'll keep your name out of any information you give us." Franco stood and gently pulled Jo up with him. "Let's go."

Lynn led them to the door. Sheehan followed, then signaled to them to stand back as he opened the door. He looked out, then with a nod that all was okay, stepped outside.

As they filed onto the porch, Lynn grabbed Franco's hand. "Franco," she said in a low voice filled with longing.

He placed his hand over hers. "Take care, Lynn."

Once they were in the car and driving away, Franco turned to Jo. "Hopefully, the South Philly address is a good lead. Otherwise, we wasted the morning." He grimaced. "I didn't want to see Lynn again, but I feel badly about what happened to her."

Pity for Lynn swept over Jo. That was one mixed-up woman. Saddled with an abusive husband, she appeared to take lovers with ease, yet the woman still carried a torch for Franco and believed herself to be in love with him based on three weeks of dating. Sounded like a soap opera. Jo wasn't a soap opera fan.

"I'll call Morelli and give him the South Philly address," she said. "He should be able to get a search warrant. DiGiacomo is wanted for the assault on Lynn and parole violation."

After her call to the detective, she tucked her phone back into her purse and turned to Franco. "Let's go over what we have so far."

"We did this already."

"We need to do it again now that there's a good chance the cops will pick up DiGiacomo. We need to make sure we don't miss anything." She edged forward in her seat and held up her hand. "First, someone ransacks your house." She began counting off on her fingers. "They appeared to be looking for something."

Franco nodded.

"Then they blow up your car, but call you right before and ask for the money. But from what Lynn said, Sal

109

wouldn't want money or anything from you other than to beat you to a pulp. Next, someone in a black Escalade drives by your house as you're coming out and takes shots at you. DiGiacomo has a black Escalade. You get more threatening phone calls, then the attack outside the restaurant, and later the rock thrown through your window. And they threaten me. Did I forget anything?"

"The note in my pocket after Susan's booksigning."

"Ah, yes." She shook her head. "DiGiacomo's asking for money doesn't add up. I'm missing something here."

Struggling to make sense of everything, Jo noticed Harris glancing into the rearview mirror, a worried look on his face. "Anything wrong?" she asked.

"We've got company," he said in a terse voice.

Jo and Franco looked out the back window. "Where? Who?" Franco asked.

"A couple of cars back. A black Escalade. Been following us the last two miles. I need to take evasive action."

CHAPTER ELEVEN

"Buckle up," Harris said, as Jo opened her jacket and slid her gun from her holster. "And hold on tight."

They were in the left lane of the three-lane highway. Harris increased his speed. The car purred along barely making a sound. When the car in front wouldn't move out of his way, Harris veered to the next lane, cutting off an SUV. Harris then swung the sedan back to the left lane to the tune of the SUV's blasting horn.

Jo twisted to look out the rear window. The black Escalade, three cars behind in the middle lane sped up also, swinging to the right lane to pass slower moving vehicles, before shifting back to the middle.

Harris increased his speed again. Jo leaned as far as her seatbelt allowed and glimpsed the speedometer. Eighty, climbing to eighty-five. The smooth ride of the car belied their speed. She glanced at Franco to find him watching her. Rather than look frightened, as she'd expected, he smiled.

"You're enjoying this," she said.

"I've gone faster. I owned a Ferrari before I wrecked it." His smile faded. "I don't enjoy someone trying to kill me though."

"Sonofabitch," Harris snarled. "Damn SOB is sticking with me. And damn these slow-moving jackasses in front of me."

Jo gripped the edge of her seat as the Town Car swerved to the middle lane and back again.

"There's an exit up ahead," Harris yelled.

"You'll never get over in time," Jo said. "There are too many cars in the other two lanes."

"Have faith in me, darlin'."

Harris gave it gas. The car shot ahead, darted to the middle lane, then back to the left. The exit loomed ahead, coming closer and closer. At the last second, in one swift maneuver, Harris managed to steer the car over three lanes of traffic to the exit. Horns blared behind him. The car fish-tailed down the exit lane. Harris fought to steady the large vehicle. It finally stabilized and Jo exhaled a relieved breath.

They sailed through the toll booth with their electronic pass. Harris looked into the rearview mirror. "We lost the SOB." He pulled into the parking lot of a strip mall and eased the car into a spot. With the car idling, he turned to them.

Franco unbuckled his belt and leaned forward, resting his arm on the back of Harris' seat. "You're a hell of a driver, man. A real pro. Good job."

Harris shrugged. "I've had some practice."

"I think my heart's stuck somewhere in my throat," Jo said.

"C'mon, Jo. Have I ever let you down?" Harris asked.

She chuckled. "No, but there's always a first time." She released her belt. "Sheesh. When I get home, I'm trading in my Corvette for a nice, staid sedan."

Franco stared at her. Jo suppressed a grin at the shocked look on his face.

"You have a Corvette?"

She shrugged. "It's my one indulgence."

"You never fail to surprise me, Fortune." His devilish

and sexy smile set her blood to boiling. "Sure that's your only indulgence?" he asked in a husky voice. "I suspect you've got a few more."

Ignoring him, she turned to Harris. "What do you think that was all about back there? Were they trying to force us off the road? Kill us? Scare us?"

"Could have been any one of those things."

"What do we do now?"

"Our friends in the Escalade will get off at the next exit and backtrack. It's what I'd do. Unless they just wanted to scare us. I'll use the GPS to get us away from the highway and through the back roads. When it looks safe, we'll get on the turnpike again."

Harris fiddled with the GPS while Jo and Franco settled back into their seats.

"You sure know how to piss people off, Callahan. DiGiacomo is one angry dude," Jo said.

"I've pissed off lots of people in my lifetime, sweetheart, but most of them haven't wanted to kill me. I've even pissed you off a few times. Do you want to kill me?" His eyes darkened and his voice deepened. "I'd rather have you want to kiss me."

She shot a look toward the front. "Don't be a jerk." He laughed as she slid to the end of the seat.

Trying to distract herself, she pulled her cell phone from her purse. "I'll call Morelli again and tell him what happened. Maybe he can contact the New Jersey State Police to be on the lookout for the Escalade now that we have a bead on where it is."

By the time they reached Philadelphia, it was late afternoon. Harris dropped them off at Franco's with a promise to be back later. They were scheduled to attend a black-tie gallery opening. Despite Jo's protests, Franco remained adamant about attending the swanky affair.

Jo dropped her purse in the entryway and faced Franco, her arms folded across her chest. "We were almost run off the road today and you still want to go out tonight."

Franco's eyes softened. "Listen, I know you have a job to do and I appreciate that. It'll be okay. Morelli's getting a search warrant for the house in South Philly. They could have DiGiacomo in custody tonight. I'll have you with me inside the gallery and Harris will be waiting outside. There will be tight security at the gallery too, with all those expensive paintings and sculptures. If I lock myself in here, then that scum DiGiacomo has won without firing a shot."

"If he kills you, he's won big time. And what about that booksigning? Someone there was working for DiGiacomo."

"Maybe, but he didn't hurt me, did he?"

"But—"

He stepped closer and put his finger to her mouth. "No buts." His voice thickened. "We've got something more important to take care of. Something I've wanted to do all day." He bent toward her.

As if her body had a will of its own, she lifted her head.

His lips came down on hers, tender and soft. She curled her arms around his neck and pressed closer to his muscular frame. He backed her up against the wall. His tongue demanded entry as one hand curved around her nape.

She uttered tiny sounds of pleasure, parted her lips, and surrendered to his demand, reveling in the feel of his mouth, his hands, and the warmth of his taut body. She drank in his scent of soap mingled with the muskiness of male arousal and met every hot, wet, glide of his tongue.

Awareness and need coalesced into a ball of molten

heat in her stomach. Her heart banged against her chest like a trapped bird. She felt like a wild creature, caged her whole life. She wanted to fly away from painful memories, from hurt. She wanted the freedom to give herself completely and unconditionally to Franco.

His hardness pressed against her belly. Moaning, she held his face between her hands as she deepened the kiss and lost herself in his taste and heat. Her body melted into his. When he finally pulled away, a small cry escaped her. Breathing heavily, he traced his finger lovingly, almost reverently, over the mole on her cheek. "I want you, Jo. So much. I know you want me too. Say it. Say you want me."

She opened her mouth to tell him what he wanted to hear, what her heart wanted. The fear and shame she'd lived with most of her life rose up to thicken her throat and cut off her words. Franco wouldn't want her when he knew the truth.

"I can't," she said on a ragged breath. She grabbed his hand and pressed his palm against her mouth, kissing him, wanting to taste him one last time. She released his hand and lowered her gaze.

He gently touched her chin, forcing her to meet his eyes. "You can't deny you want me. Trust me, Jo. I know someone hurt you." His eyes softened. "I won't hurt you. Ever. Do you believe that?"

She wanted to deny it, but she couldn't. Through misted eyes, she nodded.

"Okay, then." He bent and kissed her softly, a butterfly touch of his lips.

The sweetness of it nearly broke her heart.

As he straightened, his blue gaze bore into hers. "I'm here whenever you're ready to talk."

◇◇◇

Jo had never worn red before. Everyone always told her redheads shouldn't wear red. Everyone was wrong. Wide-eyed, she stared at herself in the three-way mirror in her bedroom, not quite believing she, Jo Fortune, was the vision in scarlet silk staring back at her.

The evening gown with the thigh-high slit and low-cut bodice hugged her every curve. She extended her leg, bared by the slit, and turned her foot, admiring the silver stiletto sandals. Mitzi had insisted the gown was perfect for her. She hadn't believed it. Until now.

Jo raised her hair off her nape, then let it fall to swish around her shoulders. In the soft lamplight, her shoulders, bare except for the thin straps of the dress, gleamed with a pearlescent sheen. Jo had never been a vain person, and wasn't about to start now. But, as she pirouetted in front of the mirror, pride surged through her. She looked good—sexy and elegant. She liked the feeling.

Tonight's gallery opening benefited a children's charity and promised to be one of the highlights of the Philadelphia spring season. The event at Rittenhouse Square, one of the city's wealthiest neighborhoods, would draw the area's glitterati. And, thanks to Franco and the beautiful clothes, tonight she'd be one of the beautiful ones.

Guilt hit her in the gut and roused the butterflies that had settled there. Tonight wasn't about her. Tonight was about keeping Franco alive.

She and Harris would have to be extra vigilant. The police had gotten a warrant to search the South Philly house where Lynn had told them DiGiacomo's mistress lived. They'd found an elderly woman, the mistress's grandmother, living there alone. There was no sign DiGiacomo had ever been there.

Thanks to Lynn, DiGiacomo knew they were on to him. And he was still on the loose.

She would protect Franco with the help of the police and the gallery owner's security force. Besides the priceless art and sculpture, the guests would also be heavily guarded, or rather, the jewels the women would be wearing would be. Including those she herself wore.

She touched the ruby pendant that perfectly complemented the silk gown. The pendant and matching drop earrings were on loan from an upscale Philadelphia jeweler. Harris and Franco had stopped to pick them up yesterday on their way home from Franco's office. She gave her reflection an ironic smile. The rich, who could afford to buy expensive jewels, had jewels loaned to them. No one would trust plain Jo Fortune with these exquisite gems if the Callahan name wasn't attached.

"Jo? Harris is here. Are you ready?"

Franco's voice outside her door started a fresh round of flutters in her stomach. "Coming." She grabbed the silver clutch from the bed and dropped her lipstick in. Her phone and Glock nestled in the satin lining.

As she took a deep, calming breath, she inhaled the flowery scent of the expensive perfume Franco had given her a few days ago. She liked the clean fragrance of jasmine with a hint of mint. She was beginning to enjoy the rarified lifestyle Franco lived too much. If she didn't get away from this place of wealth and privilege, she might not be the person she'd worked so hard to become. The thought scared her to death.

When she opened her bedroom door, Franco had his back to her and was adjusting the cuffs of his tuxedo shirt. He turned and froze. His eyes widened as he sucked in an audible breath.

"You look amazing," he managed in a husky whisper.

Heat flooded Jo's face. "Th-thanks," she stammered.

He walked toward her. His eyes glinted with admiration and something else, something that made pleasure settle in the center of her chest and flow outward through her veins like honey.

When he reached her, he took her hand and lifted it to his lips. He kissed her hand, then turned it over to draw a lazy circle in the center of her palm with his finger. He closed her fingers over her palm as if he wanted her to hold tight to his touch.

Jo forgot to breathe as Franco's hot, bold gaze locked with hers.

"I've always thought you were beautiful," he said in a thick voice. "I've wanted you from the minute I saw you at Doriana and Logan's wedding."

At his startling words, her throat constricted.

He caressed her face with a gentle touch. The feel of his warm fingers made her sway closer, wanting to absorb his heat into her body.

"It's not just your beauty," he said. "You're smart. You make me laugh. You're never boring."

Her bones turned to liquid. "You barely paid attention to me at their wedding," she said, finding her voice. "You were with some striking blonde. I'm not your type. You said it yourself."

He laughed softly. "You've always been my type, Jo Fortune. I noticed you, so much so that my date got angry. We had a huge fight over it." He leaned closer. "There's always been something about you. Something that makes me want you more than I've ever wanted anyone."

Swallowing, she backed away. "Don't say those things. Please. We have to go."

"You're right. Let's go. I want to show you off and bask in the envy of every man there." He took her arm and tucked it into his. "But we're not finished with this discussion."

"What do you think of that one?" Franco asked.

Jo sipped her sparkling cider and studied the huge marble sculpture in front of them. She turned her head, trying to get a better angle on the piece. "It's different," she said, looking up at him. "I wonder if I'm the only one who thinks it looks like a vagina?"

His arm holding his champagne flute froze halfway to his mouth. Lowering his arm, he burst out laughing. Several people turned to stare at them with disapproving looks.

"My God, Jo," he said when he stopped laughing. He snaked his free arm around her waist and drew her against him. "I never know what you're going to say. You bring a fresh perspective to everything."

"Seriously, Franco. Isn't that what it looks like?"

He laughed again. "It does."

She smiled and pressed closer to him. They'd been at the gallery almost three hours. After her initial nervousness and self-consciousness at the way everyone stared at them, she'd lost herself in the myriad display of paintings and sculptures. The gallery's openly vigilant large security force helped her relax. She'd never been into art, but she had to admit this evening was fun. She stole a glance at Franco. Having him next to her, attentive and patient as he explained some of the art, helped.

Despite her feelings of warmth and contentment, and the presence of the gallery's security detail, she was fully aware of her surroundings. Whenever anyone approached them, a member of the wait staff, a guest, or a gallery employee, her senses went into high alert. At times she felt like a pit bull, guarding her master and ready to tear apart anyone who tried to hurt him.

When they'd first arrived, Franco had had a lengthy conversation with the gallery owners, Chloe and Matteo Di-Marco, a beautiful young couple who Franco said divided their time between their house in Philadelphia and their villa in Ravello, Italy. As they talked to the friendly couple, Jo had felt unwanted twinges of envy at the obvious love between Chloe and Matteo. Deep in the recesses of her soul, Jo wanted that kind of love.

As she and Franco strolled through the rooms of the spacious gallery, admiring some of the pieces, confused by others, they spoke to artists and guests and nibbled on the gourmet food offered by the white-jacketed wait staff. Franco seemed to genuinely enjoy being with her and she found herself reveling in the thought. She looked at him and reminded herself where they were and why they were there. If only things were different.

After a while, the crowd began to thin, and they wandered more easily through the large rooms. Franco kept his hand on the small of her back as they walked. Jo inhaled the rich aromas of beef, chicken, and vegetables from the selection of food that had been served. A table in a corner of the main room overflowed with cakes and sweets, their sugary scent making her mouth water. The soft white walls and the light oak floors, polished to a high gloss, whispered wealth and privilege. She felt like Cinderella at the ball. Would the Town Car morph into a pumpkin and her prince disappear at midnight? If this prince disappeared, they'd all be in a lot of trouble.

They entered one of the smaller rooms, filled with

bronze sculptures. Franco stiffened beside her. Jo looked up at him, then followed his gaze to a well-dressed, middle-aged couple.

"Damn," Franco said under his breath.

"Who are they?" Jo asked.

"Mac's parents."

The woman, in a long white beaded gown, wore her blonde hair in a helmet-like bob. The silver-haired man with her was tall and elegant in his tuxedo. But it was the malice in the couple's eyes as they stared at Franco that set off alarms in Jo's head. She discreetly opened her purse then lowered her hand, letting the soft folds of her dress hide the gun from view. The few others in the room had drifted away, leaving Franco and her alone with the other couple.

Mac had been Franco's friend, his partner. Surely, the stylish people facing them would do him no harm.

Franco tightened his arm around Jo's waist as Mac's parents, their bodies stiff and their faces set into determined masks, strode toward them.

When the other couple reached them, Franco nodded and said, "Robert, Teresa."

"Don't waste your breath being polite," the man said.

"What are you doing here?" his wife asked in a voice sharp enough to cut glass.

The sculptures blurred and faded as Jo concentrated all her attention on the older couple.

"I'm here the same as you. At Chloe and Matteo's invitation." Franco's voice was tight with tension.

Casually, Jo slid over, putting herself between Franco and the others.

The woman, eyes flashing with hatred, stared at Franco over Jo's head.

"You should be ashamed to show your face in public," the woman spat out.

"Let's go, Teresa," her husband said. "He's not worth it." He took his wife's arm to lead her away.

"Murderer!" she shouted.

Her vile word hung in the air, tainting the rarefied atmosphere, as Teresa turned and the couple marched out of the room.

Jo furrowed her brow and turned to Franco. "What was that about? I thought Mac died in prison."

"He did," Franco said in a dead voice. "I put him there.

CHAPTER TWELVE

Franco and Jo left the gallery soon after the incident with Mac's parents. They said their goodbyes and thanks to the DiMarcos, then hurried outside and into the Town Car. Jo pressed against the door on her side of the backseat, not looking at Franco. She didn't need to look at him to feel his tension. It vibrated through the car's interior. She needed to sort out her confusion. Franco's admission had hit her like a sucker punch to the gut.

Neither of them spoke on the short ride home. When they entered Franco's house, he secured it, then headed toward the living room. Jo followed and watched as he went to the bar, pulled out a brandy snifter, then popped the top on the brandy decanter.

As he lifted the bottle of liquor, Jo put her hand over his, stopping him. He gave her a questioning look, then set down the bottle. "What?"

"We need to talk," she said. "Now. And I need you to have a clear head."

"My head's clear."

"Franco, you've been holding out on me again. I want Mac's whole story. I want to know why his parents think you murdered him." Her gaze locked on his. "And I want to know why you sent him to prison."

With a frustrated sigh, he slipped off his tuxedo jacket

and threw it over a nearby chair. "Can I at least have a glass of water?" Loosening his tie, he tossed it on the bar, then unbuttoned the first few buttons on his shirt and rolled up his shirtsleeves, exposing tanned, muscled arms sprinkled with fine dark hairs.

He looked so masculine. Her desire for him released some of the anxiety that had tightened her chest since they left the gallery. Hoping he wouldn't notice her ogling him, she waved a hand. "Yes, and bring me ice water too."

He raised an eyebrow.

"Please," she said.

"You sure are bossy." Despite the seriousness of the situation, his eyes held a glint of humor.

"You ain't seen nothin' yet." She kicked off her heels and stalked to the leather sectional and primly set her purse on the table in front of her.

Franco's soft laugh, his first since they'd confronted Mac's parents, followed her.

A few minutes later, seated next to each other, Franco lifted his water goblet, drank deeply, then replaced his goblet on the table. Not looking at her, he sat on the edge of his seat, legs apart, his arms resting on his thighs. "What do you want me to say?"

"The truth, Franco. Always the truth. Start with how you were involved with Mac going to prison."

Staring straight ahead, he said, "The same time Mac and I started the center for the kids in North Philly, we also started the charity to fund it. Mac had a degree from Wharton so he was a natural to run the charity. We hired experienced people to manage the center. It was hard work, but I was really proud of all we accomplished."

He slid back and braced an arm along the back of his

seat, then turned to look at her. "Mac's parents are wealthy. Same as mine. With our contacts, we had no trouble raising money. Although I'm a blind partner, I worked my contacts and helped organize fund-raisers." A shadow came over his eyes. "Until he was arrested, Mac's parents didn't know I was his partner. They thought he started the center and the charity on his own and were relieved Mac was finally doing something worthwhile. He'd always been wild, and had gotten heavily into drugs during his teen years. Far as I know, he was clean by the time he got to college."

Giving her a cynical smile, he continued. "Mac's parents were always traveling somewhere, without him. So whenever Mac got into trouble, they'd make it go away, and they'd make excuses for him. Then they'd be off on another trip. My parents indulged me too, but they were always there for me."

She touched his arm where it rested along the sofa back. The warmth of his skin heated her hand, and his tense muscles bunched under her fingers. "I don't understand why you didn't want anyone, especially your family, to know you were involved in the charity and youth center."

"I had my reasons. I was perfectly content to let Mac take all the credit." He pinched the bridge of his nose. "I was a fool, Jo. I gave him free rein and he screwed me. And, more importantly, he screwed the kids. I should have seen he hadn't really changed."

"What happened?"

He blew out a breath and stared at a spot above her head. "Mac stole from the charity. He embezzled close to seven hundred fifty thousand dollars."

"Oh. My. God. That's awful."

"Yeah, it is. As a partner, I should have known something was off. But I trusted him." He hunched forward, hands on his knees, and looked down at the floor.

Jo placed her hand over his. "Don't beat yourself up because you trusted a friend."

He lifted his gaze to hers. "I run a multi-national company. Although I've got good people helping run my company, I'm ultimately responsible for what happens, and I'm responsible for my employees. My department heads report to me. I know everything that goes on at the firm. Yet, Mac, my partner and friend, was stealing from the charity right under my nose and I saw nothing."

"When did this happen and how did you find out about it?" she asked softly.

He gripped her hand and held it tightly as he settled back into the sofa, his gaze still on hers. "About three years ago, Mac was on a month-long Hawaiian vacation with his latest girlfriend. It was a slow period, and Mac's assistant could handle most problems that might come up. Mac had only been gone a couple of days when his assistant called me, very agitated and concerned about a letter the charity received that day from the State of Pennsylvania. Henry, his assistant, had called Mac in Hawaii, and left a message. When Mac didn't call right back, his assistant got worried and contacted me."

"Letter?"

"A threatening letter. Apparently, not the first one they'd sent. Mac's assistant hadn't seen the other letters. Mac liked to micromanage and usually grabbed the mail before Henry saw it."

Jo rolled her neck to relieve the knot that had formed between her shoulder blades. Franco still held her hand. "What did the letter say?"

"The state threatened the charity with a cease and desist unless we allowed them to do an audit of the books."

"Audit?"

"Yeah, an audit." He settled back into his seat but didn't release her hand. "The state had gotten a complaint from a donor saying he suspected the charity might not be using the money for the kids' club. The state wanted to do an audit, and Mac ignored their requests."

"What did you do?" she asked.

"I called the state authorities and told them they could do an audit anytime. To refuse an audit is a serious offense. The auditors came the next day. I went into Mac's office with them. Our tech guy met us there too because we needed to get into Mac's computer. I looked around the office and found a credit card statement from the charity's account among some papers on Mac's desk. I was shocked to see Mac had used the charity's credit card to charge a golf membership at one of the most expensive clubs around. Alarms started going off in my head."

He closed his eyes and rubbed the back of his neck, then looked at her. "Mac's desk was locked and I couldn't find anything else, but my instincts told me there was a lot more. He'd gotten careless with the credit card bill and left it lying around. I figured I'd find more evidence if I dug deeper. And the auditors needed to see everything."

"Let me guess," she said, trying to ease the tension. "A locked desk didn't stop you."

He shot her a you-know-me-well smile that warmed her insides. "I picked the lock and found other statements showing he'd charged trips to Vegas, even charged for hookers, for God's sake, on the charity's credit card. You should have seen the looks on the auditors' faces when I handed them the credit card statements."

"Hookers? Charged to a charity for kids. That's reprehensible."

"Tell me about it." He released her hand and slid back to study her. "When I saw that I got sick to my stomach."

A thick rope of disgust coiled in Jo's stomach as well. "What did you do?"

"The auditors went over the books and took Mac's computer back to their offices. They built a good case against him. Mac finally called his assistant, but Henry was under strict orders not to tell Mac about the investigation. When he got back from Hawaii, we were ready for him."

She frowned. "Did they think you were in on the scam too?"

"They suspected me at first. Mac's assistant assured them I didn't have any hands-on dealings at the charity. I showed them the contracts Mac and I had signed stating I was a blind partner and didn't manage the charity or the kids' center. They could also see I was as shocked as they were at what we found."

He pushed up from the sofa and stood. "I need that drink now."

After he'd poured himself a brandy, he leaned against the bar and sipped his drink, his attention focused on the wall behind Jo. Fine lines of tension etched his mouth, and his skin stretched taut over his high cheekbones. She missed his closeness and his heat. She shifted in her seat, fighting the twinge of hurt that formed a hollow ache in her chest. He'd put distance between them. He wanted to be alone with his painful memories. She wanted to comfort him, but he didn't need her or her comfort.

"So, what happened when you confronted him?" she

asked finally.

He looked at her. "I wanted to talk to him alone, give him a chance to explain first. I'd hoped he had some good reason why he stole from the kids. He blew me off, said it was no big deal, that he'd repay the money. All he'd say was he'd gotten over his head with some gambling debts, and the temptation of all that money was too hard to resist. He could pay off his debts and still have plenty of money. He'd also started using again."

"Using?"

"Cocaine." Disgust flashed over Franco's face. "Besides the actual theft of the money, Mac had no idea, or didn't care, that if this had gotten out, all our good work would have been destroyed." He shook his head. "Can you see the headlines? '*Needy kids' money used for booze and hookers*'."

"I doubt that would have gone over well."

"Ya think?" His tense features belied his flippant response.

"Wasn't it in the paper anyway when he got arrested?"

"There was a little bit about it, but Mac's parents managed to keep the more damaging details out of the papers. So no one except those of us involved knows the whole truth."

He sipped more brandy, then held the glass firmly between his hands and stared at the amber liquid. "Why didn't I see it coming? After three years, I still don't have the answer."

She stood then and went to him. Maybe he didn't want her comfort, but she wanted to give it. When she reached him, she took the drink out of his hand and set it on the bar. He opened his arms and she went into them, settling herself between his legs and resting her head on his chest. He stroked a hand up and down her back.

"Mac begged me not to press charges," he said. "Promised he'd make it up to me and the charity." He pulled away. "The choice wasn't mine. Even if it was, I would have turned him in. It wasn't just me he'd hurt. He'd betrayed the kids. I couldn't forgive him for that."

"I know. You did the right thing." She placed her hands on his shoulders. "I assume they sentenced Mac to a minimum security prison."

He nodded. "His parents felt I shouldn't have called in the auditors, that I should have waited for Mac, then come to them for the money. They said I should have hushed everything up, like they'd always brushed away Mac's screw-ups. But I couldn't. I would have been at fault too if I'd covered it up. And I couldn't have lived with myself if I'd done that."

"You did the only thing you could. You said he embezzled almost a million dollars. He spent all that on golf memberships, vacations, junkets to Vegas, and hookers?"

Franco shook his head. "The auditors found bills for a quarter of that. Mac told us he'd spent it all, but we never found where he might have spent it. Whenever the authorities questioned him about the rest of the money, he clammed up. I replaced half the money out of my own funds and plan to replace the rest over time."

"Do you think he stashed it away?"

He frowned as understanding dawned in his eyes. "The money. Whoever is after me wants money. The money Mac stole? But who else knows we didn't account for it all? How would DiGiacomo know?"

The familiar rush of discovering a lead pulsed through Jo. "You said Mac died in prison. How?"

"He was stabbed."

"You don't expect murder in a country club prison."

"Prison is prison I guess. Mac could be an ass at times. He probably pissed off the wrong person."

Excited now, she pulled free. "I need to do a little research, find out who Mac's cellmate was, find out who killed Mac and why."

Franco took her hand and pulled her back into his arms. "I want to help."

"You do?"

"Of course. We're partners, aren't we?"

Her heart melted. He needed her. "I guess we are."

"Okay, partner, where do we start?"

"I need to check my resources online. What's Mac's full name?"

"Robert MacIntyre, the third."

She pulled free again and grabbed his hand, heading for her laptop. "Let's go."

"Whoa, there," he said, pulling back. "First you change into something less sexy. I can't concentrate with you looking so hot."

At the desire in his eyes, her body melted along with her heart. She kissed him lightly on the lips, grabbed her purse from the table and strode out of the room, a smile on her face. He thought she was sexy, but his willingness to follow her lead in investigating Mac acknowledged his acceptance of her security expertise. And that was sexy as hell.

CHAPTER THIRTEEN

After a fitful sleep, Jo had woken an hour ago. Now at four in the afternoon, the house was tomb-quiet. Although it was Sunday, Franco had gone to one of his construction sites. The police had caught two teens breaking into a shed where copper wire was stored. Harris, who usually spent the daytime hours of Saturday and Sunday at the house while Jo slept, had driven Franco and left a note telling Jo where they'd gone.

Restless, lonely, and missing Franco more than she cared to admit, Jo ambled into the kitchen, put her gun on the granite-topped center counter, then slid onto one of the stools. She folded her arms on the counter and stared out the back window. The shade was up, letting in the pale light of an early spring afternoon. She could see the dogwood tree, its pink blossoms beginning to wither and fall off to make way for the green leaves of summer. Kind of like her life without Franco, dried and dead, except without the promise of a bright future once she returned to Tucson.

She straightened, eyes wide. Lack of sleep was distorting her mind and causing her to think crazy thoughts. And yet, last night, held in Franco's arms after he'd told her about Mac, consoling Franco, kissing him, they'd shared a new intimacy, an intimacy as much spiritual as physical. She closed her eyes, feeling his heat wrapping around her as it had last night, his hands and mouth on her. He'd needed her, and she was glad she'd been there for him. Truth hit her like a bullet between the eyes. She had feelings for him. Strong feelings. She rested her head on her arms, her eyes closed, as if she could stop the awareness from spreading—but it was no use. She had to admit she'd been attracted to him all along, from the first time she'd seen him—cocky, arrogant and sexy—at Logan and Doriana's wedding.

She raised her head. What was she going to do now? After the lead Lynn had given them proved false, the police had gotten another lead on DiGiacomo's location. They might be bringing him in soon. If it turned out he was the perp, the threat would be over and she'd have to leave. She'd say goodbye to Franco and that would be it. A small seed of hope blossomed in her chest. Maybe he'd ask her to stay.

"Jo Fortune, you are a fool." Franco had needed her last night because his painful memories had made him feel vulnerable. Once the cops caught whoever was after him, Franco would be his old arrogant self and he wouldn't need her. Wouldn't care if he saw her anymore.

She grabbed her gun, tucked it into the waistband of her jeans at the small of her back and stalked out of the room, heading upstairs to her bedroom where she stored her gun-cleaning equipment. She'd clean her gun. That would help her focus on her mission, on the real Jo, and not this lovesick creature with the fancy clothes.

Back in the kitchen, she spread her gun-cleaning equipment on the counter and sat. But she couldn't concentrate. This whole situation had conflicting thoughts tossing around her head like leaves in a hurricane. Despite what the others thought, she was no longer sure DiGiacomo was the only one after Franco. Last night Franco and she had researched

Mac's prison record. His cellmate, a former Wall Street trader, was still in the minimum security facility. The inmate who'd killed Mac had been transferred to a more secure prison. Nothing in their research indicated anyone connected to Mac had any reason to kill Franco. DiGiacomo was the logical suspect.

And yet, something wasn't right.

There was the money. The person trying to kill Franco wanted money. Lynn had said her husband didn't need money. More than half of what Mac embezzled wasn't accounted for. Jo rubbed her aching temples against a tension headache that was beginning to throb.

She slid off the stool, poured herself a glass of water, then pulled the bottle of aspirin from the cabinet and popped three pills into her mouth. Her mind still whirling, she downed the water and pills and set the glass on the counter. In her distraction, she set the glass too close to the edge. It tottered, then fell on the tiled floor and shattered.

Damn! She'd have to clean it up. When she'd finished scooping the last of the glass shards into the dustpan, she opened the garbage can and gagged. Something was definitely ripe in there. She'd have to empty the can before it stunk up the whole kitchen.

A few minutes later, after disengaging the security system with the small remote they kept in the kitchen, she opened the back door, plastic garbage bag in one hand, her gun in the other, and cautiously peeked out. The iron garden gate was closed. Other than the twittering of birds and the soft whisper of the wind through the leaves of the dogwood tree, all was quiet. Jo hurried out to the large waste company garbage can and deposited her package, then ran back inside, locking the steel door behind her.

She placed her gun on the cleaning cloth, then washed her hands. As she bent to put a new plastic bag into the metal can, a shuffling noise made the hairs on her nape stand on end.

Straightening, she turned toward the doorway leading into the dining room—and met DiGiacomo's hard eyes. She froze, the breath sucked from her. Then she breathed deeply, filling her lungs with air, steeling herself.

"Well, what do we have here?" he snarled, an evil grin spreading on his face. His dark hair had grown out from the buzz cut he sported in his mug shot. He was bigger and more muscular than he looked in the picture. The knife he held in one hand screamed he meant business as his chest muscles bunched under his black T-shirt. Dressed all in black, he reminded Jo of a menacing bear. A bear she had to fight.

She pivoted toward the counter and her gun. He grabbed her by the arm and swung her around, slamming her, face first, into the wall, then, with his large, calloused hands, pinned her against the hard plaster. She braced herself with her hands.

"Bitch," he whispered into her ear. "I'm gonna have fun showing you who's boss."

Think, Jo, think. Put him off, buy time. "How-how did you get in here?" The adrenaline rush gave her voice a slight tremble.

He laughed, a nasty sound. "You think I'm stupid? Ain't no door in the world can keep Salvatore DiGiacomo out. I've been watching this house. It's easy, sits on the corner, sheer curtains. Saw you go out back. Knew you were alone. Piece of cake to break in while you were outside."

"What if one of the neighbors saw you? The police could be on their way now."

He pushed her face against the wall, making her grunt. "No one saw me, but if they did, I'll be gone before the police get here."

Her phone, still in her pocket, rang. She hoped DiGiacomo wouldn't make her answer it. If it was Harris or Franco or the detective, and she didn't answer, they'd know something was wrong.

"Don't even think of answering that phone," DiGiacomo said.

She swallowed. *Thank you, God.* The phone finally went silent.

"What do you want?" she asked.

His garlic-laced breath against her neck made her cough. "That pretty boy Callahan fucked my wife. No one does that and gets away with it."

"So you want to kill him for banging your wife? Kind of extreme if you ask me."

"I ain't asking you."

Anger pulsed through her, along with a big dose of fear. "Well, you're shit out of luck. Franco's not here. So leave."

His low, raspy laugh sent shivers along her spine.

"You're a feisty one. I know he's not here. Who do you think sent him on that wild goose chase?"

"The break-in at the site? That was you?"

"Some kids will do anything for a couple hits of coke."

With any luck, when she didn't answer the phone, the police or Harris and Franco would be on their way. "If you're not planning to kill Franco, why did you send him away? And why are you here?"

"I'm not gonna to kill that prick. Least not yet. I figured out another way to hurt him." He trailed the knife down the side of her face. "I'm gonna see how he likes it when another guy fucks *his* bitch." He grabbed her breast and squeezed. "I like 'em bigger, but you'll do. I guarantee once I get through with you, you won't want that pretty boy."

"Apparently your *wife* found someone else after you had her."

"Shit, bitch. When I'm through fucking you, I'm gonna cut your pretty face. See if your rich boyfriend wants you then."

Her head hurt worse than ever. The aspirin hadn't kicked in yet. She had to get control. "What makes you think Franco will care who balls me? He has a lot of women."

"Don't give me that crap. I saw you two at the wine shop. He took what was mine. I'm taking what's his."

"*You* slipped the note into his pocket?"

He pressed against her. She felt his hard erection at her back. Bile rose in her throat. She swallowed it along with the memories of other times, other horrors.

"Oh, yeah, baby," he said, rubbing himself against her backside. "A wig, glasses, uniform and everyone too stupid to notice. That waiter's probably still strung out on all the dope I gave him."

They'd really messed up. They could have had him that night. How had all three of them missed him? DiGiacomo was getting turned on. She had to shortcut him somehow. "That you in the drive-by?" She knew better than to antagonize a jerk like DiGiacomo, but if she could get him to lose his cool, she might have a chance at escaping. "If so, you're a lousy shot."

He stopped rubbing himself against her and shoved her up against the wall again, hard. "Shut up! If I'd wanted to hit him, I would have."

"And the turnpike?"

"Same deal. Just wanted to scare the prick."

And now for the big one. "So why do you want his money?

"Money? Why would I want his damn money?"

"You don't want any money?"

"What the fuck is this? Twenty fucking questions? I'm the one who—hey!"

In his agitation, he'd moved slightly, inadvertently giving her some space. Pulse racing, Jo dropped her right shoulder, loosening his grip on her, twisted around, and before he could gain control, double-punched him in the stomach.

"Fucking bitch!" he bellowed, stumbling.

Jo raced for her gun. She grabbed it and whirled on him, but before she could get off a shot, he tackled her, throwing her to the floor, face up. Her head hit the hard tile. For a second, she thought she saw stars. Her gun flew out of her hand.

He straddled her, his knees squeezing her hips. With one hand he imprisoned both hers above her head, and with his other hand he held up the knife. "I'm gonna cut you so bad even your own mother won't recognize you."

"Been a long time since my mother gave a damn about me." Jo spat in his face.

"Fuck!" He dropped the knife and slapped her. The metallic taste of blood sent a wave of nausea through her. She ran her tongue over her lips, feeling the cut, and looked him in the eye. "That all you got?"

"Like it rough, do you?" Slowly, his expression changed to a smile. With a low chuckle, he released her arms and stretched out to lie on top of her, nearly crushing her with his weight. "Feel that, baby? That's me wanting you. Like it?"

"Oh, yeah," she moaned. "Bring it on." Her arms freed, she sinuously slid them up between their bodies, grabbed his ears, pulled his face down to hers, then locked her legs around him. At his surprised grunt, she poked her thumbs into his eyes and pushed his head back. He screamed in pain. She dropped one of her hands, slipped one knee under him and flipped him over. Still screaming, he felt along the tile for his knife as Jo jumped off him and grabbed her gun from the floor.

"Make one move and you've got a bullet in your sorry ass," she said.

His screaming stopped. A split second later, pounding resonated from the front door, followed by the shouted word, "Police!" Then the sound of wood splintering and the door slamming against the wall. The slap of running feet heading to the kitchen was music to Jo's ears. Holding the gun steady, pointed at DiGiacomo's head, she allowed herself a small smile while a SWAT team, guns drawn, ran into the room.

"Drop the gun, lady, and put your hands where we can see them!" one of the cops yelled.

What? Holy cow, they thought she was the perp. Slowly, she set her gun on the counter, then raised her arms and backed away. "What took you so long?"

CHAPTER FOURTEEN

The paramedics and SWAT team had come and gone. Jo let out a long sigh, feeling the tension leave her body. She'd done no lasting damage to DiGiacomo's eyes according to the paramedics. Despite her protests that she was fine, they'd examined her also and put an antibacterial ointment on her cut lip. Detective Morelli came in as the uniforms were escorting DiGiacomo out, complaining loudly about his eyes, in handcuffs.

Jo had just finished giving her statement to the detective when Franco, followed by Harris, rushed into the house. Grabbing her hands, Franco pulled her up from the sectional and into his arms, almost crushing her in the process.

"The police called while we were at the site. When they said there'd been trouble at the house, I was afraid I'd lost you." His breathing harsh, he pressed her to him again.

Forgetting about Morelli, she rested her cheek on Franco's firm chest. Why not? It was where she wanted to be right now anyway. The rapid beating of his heart pulsed through her. His closeness and his concern flowed over her like a soothing balm and warmed her all over.

He drew away and cupped her shoulders, holding her at arm's length, studying her. "I should have been here." He reached out and dabbed a gentle finger over the cut on her lip. "That sonofabitch hurt you."

"I'm okay. Really." She searched his eyes, wanting to reassure him. "You couldn't have known DiGiacomo set you up so I'd be alone. I should have been more careful and suspected something."

"Don't you dare blame yourself," Franco said in a fierce voice. "If anyone should be blamed, it's the police."

Gripping Jo's hand, he whirled on the detective. "How could you have let this happen? I thought you were watching DiGiacomo."

Detective Morelli put up his hand. "We're sorry, Franco. We're doing an internal investigation to see where the breakdown occurred. We had men staking out the house in Delaware County where our source told us DiGiacomo was hiding. After the bad intel about the South Philly house, the judge refused to grant a search warrant without proof the suspect was there. DiGiacomo created a diversion that distracted our men. The stakeout team called me as soon as they figured out the diversion was to help DiGiacomo get away. I had a feeling he was headed here. I was clear on the other side of town, so when I couldn't reach Jo by phone, I sent the response team."

"Franco." Jo pulled on his hand to grab his attention. "Detective Morelli tried to call me to warn me but DiGiacomo had already gotten in. The police got here quickly. I'm fine and DiGiacomo's in custody. It's all okay."

He shook his head. "It's not okay, Jo. I could have lost you."

"But you haven't."

In the awkward silence that followed, the detective cleared his throat and Harris coughed. Her face heated. Feeling vulnerable and exposed, she pulled free of Franco.

Detective Morelli closed his notebook and stuffed it

into his pocket. "I think we have all we need now. We'll process DiGiacomo and start questioning him. I'll keep you posted." He nodded at Jo. "If you ever want a job with the Philadelphia police, we'd be glad to have you."

Jo held out her hand to the detective. "Thanks, Detective. Your men got here just in time."

With a smile, he shook her hand. "You had everything under control."

"That's my Jo." Harris grinned at her. "I know you can take care of yourself, darlin'. But we shouldn't have left you."

"Let's stop with the blame game," Jo said. "Bad guys are part of the job."

The detective shook Franco's hand, then Harris's, and with another nod at Jo, he left.

Quiet settled around them as Jo glanced at the splintered front door. "You can't leave that door like that," she said, turning to Franco.

"I'll call one of my construction supervisors to send over a couple of men to fix it."

Harris glanced at his watch. "Jo, how about you take a break tonight? Strong as you are, I know you're shaken. I'll take over your watch, but if DiGiacomo is our perp, we might not have to worry much longer. Just to be safe, we'll keep our backs up."

"That's right. *If* DiGiacomo is our perp," Jo repeated.

"What do you mean?" Franco asked.

"Something's bothering me about this whole thing." She began to pace.

"We've gone over this before," Franco said. "It's got to be DiGiacomo." He reached to take her hand and stop her pacing. "I don't want you worrying about that tonight. Harris will handle things while you rest."

"Harris can't stay up all night and go with you to work tomorrow."

Franco pulled her closer. "For once, listen to me and Harris. Get some rest. I'll cook up something for us while you lie down." He glanced at Harris. "Don't worry about driving me to work. I'm taking off tomorrow."

"Why?" Jo asked. "You never take off."

"You need to rest and I'm not leaving you alone."

"I can take care of myself, Callahan."

"For God's sake, woman, let someone else handle things for a change."

She opened her mouth to protest.

"Listen to him, darlin'," Harris interrupted. "He's right. I'll take your shift tonight while you sleep and while you get some rest now. I'll call Logan. Fill him in. I'm sure he'll want us on the job a little longer until we're sure the cops have their guy."

"See, it's all handled," Franco said.

"Stop ordering me around, both of you. Harris, you need your sleep. I'll stay up tonight. That's my *job*."

"I'm used to all-night stakeouts, darlin'. I need very little sleep. You know that. Once the door's fixed, I'll even patrol outside from time-to-time to make sure things are okay. I've got plenty to keep me busy."

"Fine," she snarled. "Have it your way. Both of you." With that, she stalked out of the room. Truth be told, she was exhausted. All those nights of staying awake had taken their toll. She knew Harris had a lot of stakeout experience, but she wondered if his mention of patrolling outside was to give Franco and her time alone.

No. Harris was a professional.

143

Three hours later Jo felt refreshed after a long shower, a short nap, and a delicious meal of baked salmon with jasmine rice and mixed vegetables in a cream sauce. Franco was a great cook. Delicious-looking, sexy, strong—and the man could cook. What more could a woman ask for?

As they ate, two of Franco's construction workers repaired the door. Franco had asked them to start once Jo had woken from her nap. He didn't want the sounds of hammering to wake her. Warmed by his consideration, she basked in feelings of security that lasted all through dinner.

While Harris patrolled outside now, making sure the perimeter of the house was secure, she sat at the kitchen counter and watched Franco load the dishwasher and clean up. Wearing jeans and a white T-shirt and brandishing a kitchen towel, he looked sexier than a man had a right to.

He turned and caught her staring. His mouth turned up at the corners in a smile that quickly faded. "How are you feeling?"

"I'm really okay. I could stay up tonight and keep an eye on things. Harris can go home."

He threw the towel on the counter and strode to her. "Let me watch over you for a change. I know how capable you are, but you've been running yourself ragged. Harris is willing to help out tonight."

He placed a butterfly kiss on her lips. "I want to take care of you. Okay?"

His kindness brought a lump to her throat, and she nodded. She heard the truth in his voice and recognized the resolve in his eyes. She dropped her gaze. The same weakness she'd experienced earlier threatened to overtake her again. Since her father had died when she was six, no man, except for Logan, the brother of her heart, had wanted to take care of her.

Franco touched the end of her nose in a teasing gesture. "I'll be finished here soon, then we'll go watch some TV. Unless you need to go to sleep now."

"I'm not sleepy. Mindless TV is just what I need." She needed him too, but she couldn't say that.

When Harris came back from his tour and settled in the kitchen, a bowl of candy in front of him, to work on his laptop, Jo and Franco headed upstairs to the media room. Jo laughed all the way through the comedy they'd streamed and was sorry to see it end. She glanced at Franco beside her on the plush sofa as he hit the remote and turned off the TV. When he put an arm around her shoulders, drawing her close, she snuggled into him.

"Loved the movie," she said. "Thanks. It felt good to laugh."

"I loved hearing you laugh."

Jo felt a yawn coming and tried to stifle it but couldn't.

"Time for you to go to bed." Franco stood and took her hand, pulling her up.

◇◇◇

With an evil grin, he closed her bedroom door and slithered across the room toward her. Trembling, Jo pulled the covers up to her chin. She knew what he wanted, what he'd do to her.

"Please," she whimpered. "Please."

When he got to her bed, he tore the covers from her and yanked them away. His eyes seemed to glow in the pale moonlight cascading through the windows. He crawled into the bed with her. The mattress squeaked the protest she couldn't voice. She tried to scream, but nothing came out.

He put his hand under her nightgown and rubbed her

private parts. "*You know what to do,*" *he said.* "*You know what I like.*"

She screamed.

Jo shot up in bed and clutched the comforter close with shaking hands. Her face felt wet. From sweat or tears? Her long T-shirt was bunched around her thighs.

The bedroom door flew open. Clad only in boxers, Franco burst into the room.

The sound of running footsteps on the stairs vibrated through the house, then Harris, gun drawn, raced into the room.

"What's going on?" Harris asked.

Jo clutched the comforter closer. "I had a bad dream. That's all."

Franco waved a hand at Harris. "I'll take care of her."

With a nod, Harris left the room, shutting the door behind him.

Then Franco was at her bedside. He sat down and reached for her. With remnants of her dream lingering, she shrank away from him.

"What is it, darling?" He gently brushed strands of hair from her face and hooked them behind her ear. "Everything's okay. I'm here."

Jo took a shuddering breath, forcing herself to relax. Still clutching the comforter, she leaned back on the headboard. "I'm all right now." She hated that her voice shook. "My confrontation with DiGiacomo today must have started the nightmares again. I haven't had one in years."

"Nightmares?"

She nodded.

"Tell me about your dreams."

"I can't."

"It might help to talk about it. Jo, please let me in."

She held his gaze. Could she trust him? She was so tired of carrying her burden alone.

Like the monster of her nightmare, pale moonlight reflected in Franco's eyes. But unlike in her nightmare, Franco's eyes held concern—and something else. Something that began to melt the terror of her dream.

With one hand still wrapped around the comforter, she glanced toward the window. "I try not to think about it when I'm alone. Only a few people, a few trusted people, know."

"Do you trust me?" he asked quietly.

She stared into his eyes and found what she wanted. "Yes."

His lips quirked in a soft smile and he reached out to skim a finger along her bottom lip. "Thanks for that." He loosened her hand from the bedclothes and held it firmly in his grip. "Go ahead, Jo, and take your time."

Like someone drowning, she grabbed the lifeline he offered. "I dreamt he was coming for me again." Her voice sounded small.

Franco went very still. "Who was coming for you?"

"My stepfather."

"Oh, Jo." He gathered her into his arms and rocked her. She wanted to cry, but no tears came. She hadn't cried since she was eight years old.

"Why don't you tell me about it? Maybe I can help. Okay if I…" He indicated making himself comfortable next to her.

She nodded.

He rearranged himself on the bed, then settled her against him with an arm around her shoulders. All Jo felt was numb.

She focused on a spot on the opposite wall where a modern painting hung. The vibrant colors of red, blue and green were muted in the moonlight. Like her life the day her father died. He'd taken all the brightness with him.

Would Franco still want her when he learned the truth, or would he be disgusted and reject her, like her ex-fiancé had? She wanted, needed, to unburden herself. Franco was a caring person. She'd seen the evidence of his compassionate nature and felt it deep in her soul.

With a sigh, still not looking at Franco, she began. "When I was six my father died. I loved him so much. He was always there for me, unlike my mother. My mother was an extremely beautiful woman who craved attention from men. I don't know what in her background made her so insecure. I think she looked on me as a threat, as competition. She looked at all females like that. Even as a child I felt it. My father made up for her lack of maternal instincts." Jo clenched her hand on her thigh, fighting the nausea the memories provoked. "It's been twenty-seven years and I still miss him."

Franco kissed the top of her head. "Take your time," he said gently. "We've got all night and I'm not going anywhere."

Although the memories were painful, with Franco beside her, she could do this. "When my father died, my world ended. My mother was afraid to be alone. She couldn't be without a man. Within a year she'd remarried. My stepfather was my father's opposite. My stepfather hit my mother and treated her like crap but she took it."

Jo drew shallow, calming breaths. "One night when I was eight, my stepfather came into my room while I was sleeping. I woke to find him on top of me. My mother was out with friends." A sob tore from her and she buried her face against Franco's hard chest. He pulled her closer.

"He raped you." Anger seethed in Franco's voice.

She nodded. "That's when it began."

"Oh, God, Jo." He stroked her hair. "I'm so sorry."

"He raped me continually for almost six months," she continued in a voice as barren as she felt inside. "Each time my mother was out or at work. He threatened that if I told her, he'd make her send me to a foster home." She released a bitter laugh. "I went to a foster home all right, but he didn't send me there. My mother did."

"What?"

"I finally told my mother what he'd done. She didn't believe me. So I told my teacher, who did believe me, and she told the authorities. I had to endure an awful physical, but it confirmed I'd been…been violated. Even after the medical proof, my mother didn't believe me. They arrested my stepfather."

"You were so brave, Jo. The sonofabitch can't hurt any more kids."

She pulled back to look up at Franco. His eyes held fury, sadness, and understanding, but no disgust. "He told my mother and the police that I'd seduced him."

"Oh, for the love of—"

"I was *eight years old*!"

Franco rubbed a hand down her back until she stopped sobbing. When she finally gained the courage to look into his eyes again, she found his face ashen in the moonlight.

He pulled her to him, holding her with tenderness, as if he thought she'd break. "I'd never hit a woman," he said, his voice low with fury, "but I'd have a hard time controlling my temper around your mother. Is the sonofabitch still in jail?"

"I hear he's out now and back with her." Franco didn't let go of her as she continued. "Soon after he was arrested, she gave me up to the state. She said I was a liar. Said she couldn't trust me. She didn't want me anymore. I spent the next ten years in foster care."

Gently, he smoothed her hair. "You didn't have any relatives who could have taken you?"

"No. My dad had a brother somewhere but they'd been estranged for years. My grandparents were dead, and my mother was an only child."

"Poor Jo."

She drew back. "I don't want your pity."

"It's not pity. I care for you. I'm sad for the child you were and in awe of the strong woman who overcame all that."

Jo didn't know what to make of that. "Sometimes I wonder how much I have overcome it." She looked around, feeling lost.

Franco gathered her to him again and kissed her tenderly on the forehead, then released her. "Don't ever sell yourself short. You're a hell of a woman, Josephine Fortune."

"Thanks, I guess." She leaned her shoulder against the headboard and leveled her gaze at him. "I've got to get it all out. If I stop now, I'll lose my nerve." Her thin T-shirt was no barrier against the April chill that permeated the room. Shivering, she folded her arms across her chest.

He reached down, pulled the bedclothes up, and covered them both.

Jo shimmied closer until they touched thigh-to-thigh. His heat warmed her heart and her body. With him so close she could fight the demons. "Some of my foster homes were okay," she continued. "They treated me well enough, but I never forgot I didn't belong with those families. I never stayed in one home very long. I acted out and got into trouble, minor scrapes at school or with the law. The foster parents said I was too angry and they didn't want to handle me. When I was seventeen, my foster father tried to rape me."

She released a harsh laugh. "Just like they all do, he said he was giving me what I wanted, that I'd been coming onto him—but this time I fought back. I knocked him over the head with a lamp and kicked him as hard as I could. He ended up in the emergency room. His wife didn't believe my story, just like my mother. She said I was a slut, claimed I went after her husband. She wanted me prosecuted for assault."

Jo slid the comforter down to her waist and picked at the ends, not looking at Franco. "The family court judge took pity on me. He arranged for me to live with him and his wife and do community service rather than go to juvie. I stayed with them almost a year until I turned eighteen." With a small smile, she looked up at Franco. "They were wonderful people. I'm still in touch with them."

With exquisite gentleness, he skimmed his finger over the mole on her face. "I'm glad you found some good people. What did you do when you were eighteen?"

"I joined the Army. That's where I met Logan. He'd been Special Ops, but was working as a trainer on our base." She rubbed a hand over her eyes as another painful memory spiked through her. "I fell in love with another enlistee, Jimmy McKee. He promised we'd get married as soon as we were out of basic. I told myself Jimmy would give me all I ever wanted—a home, family, love. Turned out he was a scum, but if it wasn't for him, I wouldn't have gotten to know Logan."

She looked down. "I couldn't relax enough to enjoy

sex with Jimmy. He said I was frigid. I figured if I told him my story, he'd understand why I found sex so…so unfulfilling, and he'd learn to be gentle and patient with me. So I told him everything. He wouldn't touch me after that, wouldn't have anything to do with me."

She raised her gaze to Franco. "Just like the others, deep down Jimmy blamed me for what had happened, that somehow being raped was my fault. How can that be?"

Franco reached for her, but she waved him away. "No. I need to finish. Right after Jimmy broke up with me, I was so upset I couldn't concentrate on my training. I kept screwing up. Logan took me aside and asked what was going on. Maybe it was the sadness in Logan's eyes that made me think he'd understand. I told him Jimmy had rejected me and why."

She gave Franco a small smile. "I won't repeat the names Logan called him. Jimmy hadn't done anything against Army rules so Logan couldn't officially punish him, but after that day, Logan rode Jimmy hard, making him do his routines over and over. It was fun to watch. I knew then Logan would always have my back. He never judged me and he treated me with respect.

"Logan saved my life. He's the brother I never had. Even when his enlistment was up, he kept in touch. I knew I could always call on him if I got into trouble. He and the Army changed me. No man messes with me now."

"Don't I know that."

A laugh bubbled up in her. Her body felt lighter, as if an immense weight had dropped off. She felt her strength return as she sat up, spine straight.

"Did you and Logan…did you ever?" he asked.

Her laugh died and she frowned. "God, no. The guy's

a hunk and all that, but I just told you he's like a brother. That's all he's ever been to me, a big brother. And besides, he was carrying a torch for Doriana. I realized later his eyes were sad because he still loved her and thought he'd lost her forever." She smiled. "His eyes aren't sad anymore."

"Logan and Doriana are one of the happiest couples I know." Franco said. "But we're talking about you now. I want to know all I can about you, Jo Fortune."

"You mean Misfortune."

"What?"

"I got teased in school a lot. The kids called me Jo Misfortune."

He kissed her, a soft kiss, gentle as a whisper. "I'll never call you that."

"I know." She moved closer, and he put an arm around her shoulders, pressing her against his side.

"When you got out of the Army, you went to work for Logan?" he asked.

"I did."

"You don't see your mother anymore?"

"She's dead to me. She would have let that filthy scum abuse me all he wanted so long as I didn't tell anyone and she didn't lose her man." Jo's eyes misted over despite her best intentions. No matter how much time passed, the pain of her mother's betrayal and abandonment was still raw. "She gave away her own *daughter*." Jo choked back her tears. She wouldn't lose it again. Not now. Not in front of Franco.

"Jo, sweetheart. It's okay to cry. I'm here for you now." Franco gathered her closer, holding her against his chest.

His crooning tone was her undoing. The tears returned then, huge drops rolling down her face and onto his bare chest. Sobbing uncontrollably, she wound her arms around his neck and welcomed the cleansing tears.

"Go ahead, darling," he whispered. "Let it all out."

CHAPTER FIFTEEN

Jo opened her eyes and took a deep breath as she stretched her sore muscles. The sweetly pungent aroma of bacon cooking teased her nostrils. Her stomach rumbled in response. She rolled over, rubbing her eyes against the sleep that remained and let the memory of the night before wash over her like a gentle rain.

The last thing she remembered was being held in Franco's arms as he soothed her troubled spirit. Consequently, she slept better than she had in months, maybe years. She looked at the other pillow and wondered if he'd stayed the night with her. Like shadows poking through mist, hazy memories of his warm body beside hers as she slept floated into her mind.

She rolled onto her side again and touched his pillow, running her fingertips over the imprint Franco's head had left on the soft cotton cover. She'd really slept curled in his arms. His signature scent of sandalwood lingered on the pillow. She smiled.

A new, disturbing thought intruded and her smile faded. In the light of day, would Franco be disgusted at what she'd told him? Would he judge her as dirty, as damaged goods, like her foster father, like Jimmy? She was strong. She'd survive. Tears pooled in her eyes and she blinked. She thought she had no tears left after last night. She glanced toward the bedside clock. Ten o'clock!

Jo threw back the covers and leapt out of bed. She hurried to her bathroom to freshen up, then slipped on a T-shirt and a pair of sweatpants and her old loafers. Holding her gun, she ran down the stairs and followed the mouth-watering bacon scent.

She froze in the kitchen doorway and drank in the sight of Franco at the stove cooking eggs and bacon. Dressed in a black T-shirt and black jeans and wielding a spatula, he looked hotter than the flame under the griddle.

He must have sensed her behind him because he turned with a smile. Mingled with the desire in his eyes was something else—something that made her heart beat faster.

"Good morning, Sleeping Beauty," he said.

Her stomach rumbled again but she ignored it. "You shouldn't have let me sleep. Poor Harris. He's been up all night." The words poured from her, harsher than she'd intended.

With a soft laugh, Franco turned away to slide the bacon and eggs onto a plate. He set down the spatula and held the plate out to her. "Not a morning person? Have some coffee. Sit. Eat. Stop worrying." He glanced at the gun she held at her side. "I don't think you need that right now."

Lured by the scent of coffee, eggs and bacon, she moved into the room and laid her gun on the counter. "I have a job."

He set the plate on the counter, studying her with softened eyes. "How are you feeling? You okay?"

She swallowed. "I'm good. Great, in fact. Thanks for everything, Franco, for listening to me, for letting me cry. I'm sorry I was so short with you a minute ago."

He came to her and cupped the curve of her jaw with

his strong hands. "It's okay, sweetheart. I'm here for you whenever you need to talk. I've got a tough hide. The important thing is that you're okay."

A small bud of hope began to blossom in her heart. She didn't see any revulsion in his eyes, or hear even a hint of it in his voice. She saw and heard only softness and caring. Holding his gaze, she touched his hands that still cradled her face. "The important thing is that we keep you safe. Where's Harris? Is he outside patrolling? I need to tell him he can go home now."

"Sit." He pulled away and gestured her to one of the stools. "Harris had breakfast and left an hour ago."

"And you let me sleep?"

"It's okay. A patrol car's outside. Morelli sent it over, but it was Logan's idea."

"You've been busy." Head spinning, Jo sank onto the stool. Franco slid the plate of bacon and eggs closer. The toaster popped up two slices, and he turned to butter them.

He set a steaming mug of coffee and a plate with the buttered toast in front of her, then pulled out a stool and sat. "Eat," he said, snagging a piece of toast for himself.

Her empty stomach protested with another rumble, and she pressed a palm against it. She couldn't remember the last time she'd eaten. They were safe for now. A patrol car was outside. Forcing herself to relax, she dug into the delicious breakfast.

Later, her stomach full, she pushed the empty plate away.

Franco's lips quirked in a smile. "You were hungry."

"Thanks for breakfast. It was delicious." She sighed. "I'm not hungry now and I need answers." She needed answers about more than her protection of Franco. She was as disarmed about her feelings for him as she'd been while grappling with DiGiacomo. But she was still a professional and personal questions would have to wait.

"Start talking," she said. "Why is a patrol car outside and what does Logan have to do with it?"

"I woke up about six and came downstairs to think," he began.

"You should have woken me."

"You looked so beautiful and peaceful. A princess. You needed to sleep."

Her face burned. She looked away, gathering her emotions close. Feeling more in control, she turned back to him. "I'm no princess and I'm here to keep you safe. Now keep talking. What did I miss?"

He got up and poured himself a cup of coffee, taking his time fixing it, then settled back onto his stool. He took a sip of his drink before setting the cup down and turning to her.

"Why can't you move and talk at the same time?" she demanded. "Talk."

"Impatient, aren't you? Morelli called me about seven. They'd been questioning DiGiacomo for hours. He admitted to the things he told you yesterday—the drive-by, to putting the note into my pocket at the wine store, and following us on the turnpike. But he won't admit to any of the more serious things—claims he never made the threatening calls or asked for money and that he knows nothing about the attack outside the restaurant, the rock thrown through the window or the bomb placed in my car."

Chills chased up her spine. "I knew it. There's someone else involved. You're still in danger."

"We're not so sure about that. Morelli thinks DiGiacomo might be denying some of the heavier stuff to bargain for a lighter sentence, but he's not willing to wager our lives on it. And Logan agrees. DiGiacomo's already in a hell of a lot of trouble for his attack on you. He doesn't want the other stuff pinned on him too."

"I don't buy it. Something isn't right. Why the police car? I thought the police were short-staffed. Besides, Harris and I are your security team."

"After I spoke with Morelli, Harris called Logan and we all talked it over. If someone else is involved, we agreed we should try to flush him out."

Franco took Jo's hand and held it in his warm grip, his eyes serious. "I don't like the idea of putting you in any further danger. I fought them on that part of the plan, but even Morelli thinks it's a good idea."

"I don't run from danger, Franco. Logan knows what he's doing. I'm not afraid."

"But I'm afraid for you."

"Don't be."

He smiled. "Look at what you did to DiGiacomo."

She returned his smile. "You should see me when I really get started. Now explain how we're going to flush out the other perp, if there is one."

"The police have already let the neighbors know they've got the guy who's been after me, but as a precaution, they're keeping a patrol car there today. Morelli had his sources spread the word on the street. We figure with the patrol car so prominent and the word on the street, if there is another perp, he'll think he's free to make his play as soon as the car's gone."

She slid her hand from his and frowned. "We all sit around and wait for something to happen?"

"If there's someone else after me, we think he'll make his move in the next day or two. The police are going to run regular patrols along the street, Harris will still guard me at work, and you'll be here. We go about our business as usual."

He leaned closer. "I insisted on more patrols than Morelli wanted to give. The promise of a big donation to the police benevolent fund helped."

"Money talks," she said with a shake of her head. "What if nothing happens in the next day or two?"

"The police will continue to grill DiGiacomo, but if things stay quiet, Morelli feels certain that will mean DiGiacomo is our only guy."

"If there is anyone else involved, I suspect they might be smarter than we think. Why wouldn't they wait us out?"

He stood. "No more questions for now. The police are handling things today. You need to rest. We'll worry about tomorrow then."

She let him take her hand and help her up. They stood a whisper apart. His clean, soapy scent reached out to her, warming her all over. Her fingers itched to touch the dark stubble on his face and trace the line of his full lips.

"I don't want to rest." The huskiness of her voice surprised her.

His blue eyes darkened to midnight. "What do you want?"

"Make love to me, Franco."

Surprise, desire, elation chased across his face. "Are you sure DiGiacomo didn't hit you on the head?"

"I wasn't hit on the head, my thoughts are very clear, and your hearing is fine. I know what I want."

Staring down at her with an expression of wonder, he

gathered her into his arms and buried his face in her hair. "I want you, Jo. I have for a long time. Are you sure? I'd never do anything to hurt you."

"More sure than I've been about anything in my life," she whispered. "And I know you would never hurt me."

He pulled away and held her at arm's length. "Jo." The way he said her name, filled with raw yearning and need, made her heart stutter with joy. He skimmed a finger over the cut on her lip. "Does this hurt?"

"I don't care if it does. I want you."

Taking her face between his hands, he kissed her softly, sweetly, careful of her cut lip. She didn't want soft and sweet. Her hunger and craving for him exploded, sending shock waves of longing through her. With a small moan, she pressed against him, melding her body to his strong frame.

He kissed her long and hard until her senses reeled and her legs turned to jelly. The pain from her cut was nothing compared to the desire that swept her. He released her, but held her hands tightly as if he were afraid she'd run away. "I've wanted you for so long."

"I'm here and all yours."

Holding onto her hand, he started to pull her from the kitchen. She grabbed her gun from the counter. At his raised eyebrow, she shrugged.

He led her through the dining and living rooms and up the stairs. When they reached the second floor, he pulled her into his room, then folded her into his embrace and kissed her temple. "If you knew what you do to me." He stared at her with hooded eyes. "You're not afraid? I'll do whatever you want. I'll stop if that's what you want."

Old fears surfaced. She shoved them aside. "Love me. Please."

161

Taking her hand, he led her to his king-sized bed. Covered in dark green silk, it dominated the room. She'd done a quick check of his suite the day she'd moved in, but hadn't been in it since. The walls of the spacious room were painted a soft cream, the furniture modern and sleek. She set her gun carefully on the nightstand next to the bed.

Franco drew back the comforter, then turned and brushed his fingers over her face. His eyes smoldered. His masculine scent filled her and loosened the knot of anxiety in her stomach.

Unable to look away from his sinful gaze, she splayed her palms on his chest. The rapid beating of his heart against her palms vibrated through her as he slipped a hand beneath her fall of hair and massaged her nape. He ran a finger gently over her lips, then dipped his head and claimed her mouth in a fervid kiss that sent fire shooting through her veins.

His tongue teased and cajoled until she opened to him. He tasted of coffee and bacon and desire. Her body felt boneless, hot, needy. Her breasts swelled and tightened. A strangled groan escaped her.

He drew away and reached for the hem of her T-shirt. With gentle, sure fingers he slipped it over her head and threw it on the floor. He stepped back and gazed at her. Her nipples hardened and puckered under his scrutiny, as if begging for his touch.

"You are so beautiful." He reached out and filled his hands with her breasts, caressing and kneading, his touch scorching. The raw hunger in his eyes fed an answering hunger in her, a craving for more than his body—for his soul.

She grasped his upper arms, afraid her legs would give out under the onslaught of pleasure and longing he incited in her.

When he bent to take one of her nipples into his mouth, she gasped and gripped his arms tighter. He massaged her breast and swept his tongue over each erect nipple. The air around them thickened, heavy with desire.

His breathing labored, he pulled away. "You should never wear a bra." His eyes softened and his voice held wonder. "Your breasts are too beautiful to imprison."

She laughed softly as pleasure swirled through her. He'd said her body was beautiful. She'd never believed that before.

His sizzling gaze still on her, he slid her sweats down her legs. She slipped out of her loafers, kicked them away, and stepped out of her pants. Franco spanned her waist with his hands and drew her closer.

He knelt before her, and with agonizing slowness, he kissed her midriff, nipping and licking her sensitized skin. He laved her navel, and hooking a finger into the waistband of her bikini panties, he removed them and tossed them aside. He stood slowly and ran his hands up her sides. Thrill, desire, need hummed through her, along with a small dose of anxiety. No man had ever looked at her with such longing and worship. She wanted only to please him. She had so little experience. Would she disappoint him?

All thoughts fled as his eyes, hot as molten lava, searched hers. Electricity charged between them. Her body on fire from embarrassment and lust, she folded her arms across her chest.

"You trust me?" he asked.

She could only nod.

He moved her arms to her sides. "Then don't ever hide yourself from me. Let me look at you. You're sure you're not afraid?"

"As long as I'm with you, I'm not." The truth of her words jolted her. Could he see the trust in her eyes?

With a smile, he scooped her up and carried her to the bed, laying her smoothly on the soft cotton sheets. He quickly undressed until he stood before her in all his magnificent, naked glory. She sucked in a breath at his sculpted beauty, at the finely honed muscles of his chest, his trim waist and long legs. His erection, thick and hard, told her more than words how much he wanted her.

His blue gaze consumed her as he got onto the bed beside her. The mattress sank under his weight. When he pulled her into his embrace, she raised her face for his kiss. Their tongues sparred in a fierce, primal duel that threatened to make her world spiral out of control. Franco slid his hands down her spine to cup her buttocks. His penis pressed against her belly.

Fire swept along Jo's skin and through her veins. Liquid warmth wet her most private parts. Wanting more, wanting all of him, she squirmed, pressing closer, wishing she could absorb his very essence.

"Take it easy," he crooned. "We've got plenty of time."

He settled his hard-muscled body over her. Passion tightened his features as he stared down at her. Aching for him to fill her, she held out her arms.

"You're mine, Jo," he whispered as he bent to take her lips in a deep, drugging kiss. Every touch of his hands and mouth told her she belonged to him. She wound her arms around his neck and surrendered to him, giving him her body and her soul.

She tunneled her hands through the thickness of his hair and shivered at the rush of warmth to her lower abdomen. He left her mouth to trail burning kisses along her jaw and the column of her throat, making his way down her body with deliberate slowness. He suckled one nipple, massaging her breasts, his mouth and tongue wicked and seductive. Crazy with desire, she grabbed his shoulders, sinking her nails into his firm flesh, writhing under him.

When his mouth found her mound, he kissed her there with tenderness, then stroked the sensitive nub. She bucked and released a low groan. He slipped fingers into her wetness, exploring, sinking deeper into her folds. Jo closed her eyes and clutched the sheets, lost in Franco's heat and passion.

"Look at me," he rasped. "I want to see your eyes when you come."

She looked at him then and gasped at the exposed emotion in his eyes—desire and lust, but also longing, as if he bared his soul to her. Then she had no more time to think as his fingers moved faster and faster inside her and she gave herself over to him. Her climax built in undulating waves, higher and higher, until she drowned in ecstasy.

She screamed as her climax shattered what little control she had. Her body trembled with the force of her release, a release that seemed to go on forever. Finally, spent, she quieted.

Franco kissed her lips and brushed hair back from her face. "You're wonderful," he whispered.

She stroked his face. "So are you," she breathed.

Placing a quick kiss on her cheek, he slid away to sit on the edge of the bed. He opened the nightstand drawer and rummaged through it until he pulled out a foil-wrapped package. After he pulled on protection, he turned to her again and settled himself between her legs.

"I want you," he said.

"Please."

He slipped easily into her. She gave herself over to the sensation of Franco filling her completely, of his possession, one she willingly bestowed. She clung to him, immersed in his scent of male and arousal. Her all-consuming need for him was a balm, cleansing her tortured soul. Need, deep and yearning, pulsed through her. She felt the same need in him, two souls reaching through the darkness to cling together. He filled her body and the hollow places in her heart. She would not allow herself to look beyond this moment.

They rocked together. She met his every thrust, faster and faster until there was nothing in her world but Franco. Her soft moans filled the room. Finally, she cried out and clung to him as another orgasm swept through her. He shuddered with his own climax, saying her name on a tortured breath. They lay still, wrapped in each other.

Hot tears pricked at her eyes. She knew she'd come home.

CHAPTER SIXTEEN

The pearly fingers of dawn broke into the room, muting the corners in soft shadows and touching the sharp planes of Franco's face. He was beautiful, even in sleep. Jo propped herself on her elbow and stared at him. He looked younger, more open, a man she could trust. She reached out to touch, then hesitated, fearing what she felt for this man. She pulled her hand away.

With a deep sigh, she rolled onto her back. She touched her lips and ran her hands over her sore and swollen breasts. The memories of what she and Franco had done with each other yesterday morning, then again through the night and into the first hours of this morning played out in her mind. Each time they made love, she'd become bolder. Her passion for him overwhelmed any lingering fears. A skillful lover, Franco had taken care of her needs first, bringing her to climax over and over. Sensual and giving, passionate and loving, he'd taught her how to please him and broke down the barriers that had kept her from fully embracing her sexuality.

Who would have thought it? Spoiled playboy Franco Callahan—a tender, unselfish lover who cared more about her pleasure than his. She was sure she'd come to know the real Franco these past weeks. Yet, he'd hidden his true nature under a playboy façade. She needed to know why.

The mattress shifted, then she was folded into Franco's

embrace. "Morning, sweetheart." He kissed her, his lips soft as a spring morning. "I'd like to wake up to you every day."

His words and his husky, sleep-filled voice made joy and hope sweep over her in waves of warmth. She wondered if he could love her. And still more, if she would be able to hold onto the completeness, the fulfillment, he had brought her. Or would it slip away as the dawn evaporated in the harsh light of day?

She had no time for further thoughts. His lips brushed hers again in a toe-curling kiss. His heat seared her, and she opened for him, wanting to devour him. His tongue joined hers in an ancient, erotic dance that left her breathless.

With a moan, he dragged his mouth from hers and crushed her against him, burying his face in her hair. "Jo," he murmured, the word filled with longing.

He made love to her then with a wildness that fed her deep craving. It felt as if they were both trying to capture something elusive, something they might never find again.

Afterward, spent, their breathing shallow, they lay in each other's arms. The room had brightened as dawn shifted to morning. Soon Franco would leave for work and she'd be alone with her hopes, dreams, and fears.

"I hate to leave you," he said, echoing her thoughts. He kissed behind her ear, making her sigh with contentment, then turned her to face him. "Let's go to dinner tonight. I know a great little place in South Philly. Very casual. It won't be part of our so-called masquerade. It will be us—two real lovers enjoying each other. What do you say?"

She touched his lips with gentle fingers. "It sounds wonderful. But I'm still on duty. Harris will have to drive us, and we need to be careful. We don't know what the next few days will bring."

Anxiety flitted over his features. "I worry about you."

"Don't. I'm just doing my job."

He grinned ruefully. "I know. But I worry anyway. When this is over, I'm taking you away somewhere exotic and isolated where I can give you champagne, feed you strawberries and make love to you for days."

"Sounds heavenly." She laughed softly. Her laughter ended as a familiar sadness surged through her. How long before he became bored with her? She'd never known him to stay very long with any woman. And she had never had a truly fulfilling relationship, had never thought she could have. She didn't know where to begin or how.

She blew out a breath. "Before you have to get ready for work, I want you to tell me something."

"Anything, sweetheart." He sat up, propped his pillow against the headboard, and leaned back. "What do you want to know?"

She straightened and sat beside him. Drawing the covers over her breasts and under her arms, she locked her gaze with his. "I've gotten to know you pretty well these past weeks. You're no spoiled playboy. Not anymore, if you ever truly were."

He shot her a wicked smile. "Oh, I was every bit the player. But those days are behind me."

"Something tells me what I'm seeing now is the real Franco Callahan, that the other was a part you were playing. Am I right?"

"Partially."

"Why the party guy image? That's not the real you. Why did you act that way?"

"You really want to know?"

"I want to know everything about you."

Light gleamed in his eyes. "Why do you want to know all about me, Jo?"

"I'm asking the questions now. You haven't answered them."

"Feisty as ever." He kissed the top of her head and settled her against him. "I can't say I didn't enjoy being a player, being one of Philly's most eligible bachelors. But you're right, and very astute. I adopted the persona as more of a defense."

She pulled away and frowned at him. "Defense?"

"Yeah, crazy as it seems. I've done a lot I'm ashamed of, and the blame is all mine. I've had it easy. My parents indulged my every wish. I was the golden boy." His eyes clouded. "The gold was tarnished though, at least in my mind. No one, not my parents, not Doriana, not Nonna, ever thought I'd amount to anything."

She smoothed her hand over his arm. "I know your family means a lot to you, especially your grandmother. Why would they think you wouldn't amount to anything?"

He stared across the room, his profile sharp and his jaw tight. Jo suspected raw memories weighed on him. He hunched his shoulders defensively, took a deep breath, and looked her straight in the eye. "Doriana and I went to a private high school. She worked hard and was on the honor roll every semester. She was the true golden girl. I couldn't compete with that so I didn't try. It was easier that way.

"I got in with a bad crowd. We partied, drank, didn't care about school. When I messed up so badly and almost flunked out, even when I got into trouble with the law, Nonna told me not to worry. She said it didn't matter what I did. That I didn't have to get good grades, that no one expected too much from me. Callahan Construction would be mine anyway. I've always loved my grandmother and her words crushed my soul. I know she meant well, but I'd felt as if my world had been kicked out from under me." He released a deep breath and pulled Jo closer.

"Doriana worked her tail off at school, then for the company, but Dad never appreciated her," he continued. "It didn't matter how much I screwed up, in high school, in college, at the company, Dad was going to pass it to me."

"So you could mess up all you wanted and everything would belong to you anyway?"

"You got it."

"So you ran with it. Some guys would think that was heaven."

"For awhile I did too. You know how I partied, the women I went out with." He pulled slightly away and looked down at her.

Jo rolled her eyes. "Yeah, I know."

He took her hands in his. "I told you before that one of the reasons I went out with the women I did was because they never expected anything from me other than a good time and expensive gifts. They bored me."

"Have you ever been in love?" The words slipped from her.

He leaned over and kissed her. "Not yet. You could never bore me, Jo. And I suspect you'd never put up with the old me, the womanizer."

Her heart began to thump wildly, the sound pounding in her ears. Maybe she was foolish to hope he could love her.

"Are you telling me you behaved the way everyone expected because it was easy?" she asked.

"Something like that."

"That's kind of stupid."

"Ya think? But I had a hell of a good time for a lot of years."

She studied him. "Franco Callahan, you don't fool me. You were hurt that no one in your family, especially your grandmother, thought you'd amount to anything. So you hid your hurt behind a player image."

"Now we're practicing psychobabble, are we?" The teasing note in his voice took the edge from his words.

"I understand people. That's what makes me a good security expert."

He took her into his arms and held her tightly against his chest. "Jo Fortune, you are so much more than that to me. My life is different now, and I'm glad. Opening the youth center was the beginning of my road to redemption. I'm sorry my dad had the stroke and I wish he were as vibrant as he used to be, but his illness forced me to man up, to grow up. If I didn't take over the company, we would have gone under. I felt I had no choice but to do it."

He kissed her temple. "Of course, my dad doesn't want to give up the controls. He calls me every day at work, insists I send him weekly reports. Maybe someday he'll have faith in me." A tinge of hurt colored his voice.

She freed herself and locked her gaze with his, hoping he could see her trust in him in her eyes. "I'm sure your dad has faith in you. He's struggling with his loss. The stroke cost him a lot. Give him time." She took Franco's face between her hands. "As I've suspected, you're a caring man with a good heart."

"I'll tell you something else. I have a powerful need for you."

In response, she wound her arms around his neck. Her heart melted along with her body and she gladly gave herself to him.

◇◇◇

Jo hummed softly as she eased the designer jeans over her hips, zipped and buttoned them. They were tight, but the touch of spandex in the fabric made them easy to move in. She dug through the lingerie drawer of the small bureau built into the walk-in closet and pulled out her white lace pushup bra, the one that matched the thong she wore.

Remembering Franco's words about her not wearing a bra, she hesitated before she snapped it on. She couldn't go braless while they were at dinner, but when they got home, she'd sure take off the confining piece of lace. Or give Franco the pleasure. She smiled, shivering at the thought.

Still humming, she sifted through the padded silk hangers in the closet until she found the silver-gray sweater, perfect for a cool spring night. She slipped on the sweater, the cashmere soft as a cloud. Her whole body tingled from Franco's lovemaking. She couldn't quite believe they'd made love one more time before he left for work. He'd turned her into a wanton and she loved it. But she was his wanton, only his.

Smiling, she left the closet, walked into the bedroom, and sank onto the bed. Was this what being in love felt like? This feeling of floating on air, wanting to laugh out loud and hug herself with happiness? She'd had no idea making love could be spiritual. That's what it had been with Franco—spiritual and otherworldly. She'd lost herself in him.

And she'd missed him all day, couldn't wait to see him tonight. She glanced at the clock. He'd be home soon. They'd go to dinner, be together. She frowned. Until they either confirmed DiGiacomo was the one after Franco, or found who was, she was on duty. No more lovemaking until her assignment was over. The patrol car was no longer parked in front of the house. She was back on the job.

Sighing, she rubbed her bottom lip. Franco said after this was over, he'd take her somewhere exotic where he could make love to her all day. Warmth rushed through her at the thought.

But that was in the future. She needed to finish dressing, then do another run-through of the house to make sure it was secure. She wiggled her bare toes. The silver stiletto sandals would go well with her outfit. Where had she put them?

Standing in the large walk-in closet again, Jo pulled out the shoe boxes lined up on shelves, searching for the shoes she wanted. She spied the silver ones, out of their box and tucked in a corner. She must have tossed them there the last time she wore them.

She bent to pick them up. The heel of one shoe was caught on a wooden floorboard that protruded slightly. Jo yanked the shoe free and landed on her backside from the force. When she sat up, she noticed the floorboard had worked itself free, leaving a gaping hole.

She crawled on hands and knees to the opening. A package, wrapped in blue silk, lay in the hole. Trepidation swept over Jo as she gingerly reached in and retrieved the packet.

Holding the silk-wrapped bundle, she stood and walked to the bed. Once seated, she placed the packet on her lap and carefully peeled away the blue silk, exposing a canvas bag like the ones banks used to transport money.

Hands shaking, she opened the bag and drew out bundles of money. God, no, please. It couldn't be. She spread the packs on the bed and stared down at them, as if she could somehow will them away. The implications of her find were too terrible to bear. She did a quick count of the packs of one-hundred dollar bills.

A half million dollars.

Mac's missing money?

In Franco's house.

She put a hand to her mouth. Did Franco know about the money? If he knew, he'd lied to her all through this situation. Even his lovemaking was a sham. His reformed playboy persona was a lie. All of it, lies.

No. No. She bit down on her lip. Her career had made her a good judge of a person's character. She couldn't be that wrong about Franco. She couldn't love him if he weren't the man she thought he was.

Blowing out a breath, she pushed off the bed and paced the room, her mind whirling with images starting from the day she'd stood in his office, resentful of the assignment, yet oddly happy at the prospect of working with him. She saw his eyes, heard his voice, felt his hands and mouth on her body. Saw the regret in his eyes when he talked about Mac, when he talked about how his family hadn't expected much of him. The man she'd come to know and love was no liar. She loved Franco. She had faith in him. They'd talk when he came home. When she told him about the money, she'd gauge his reaction, watch his face.

There had to be a good explanation for the money. He couldn't have known it was hidden in her closet.

Her phone rang once, then stopped. She ran to the night table and picked up her cell. A missed call from Harris registered. She frowned. Her phone beeped, signaling a text message. *On way*, she read. Harris must have decided a text was faster than calling.

She stuffed the money back into the canvas bag, covered it with the blue silk and pushed everything back into the hole in the closet. She set a couple of shoe boxes on the loose floorboard. She didn't want Franco to see the money before she talked to him.

Twenty minutes later, Jo heard the jangle of keys at the front door. She shoved her gun behind her in the waistband of her jeans and raced down the stairs, glad she hadn't put on the stilettos yet, then disengaged the alarm. The door swung open. The smile she had for Franco faded.

CHAPTER SEVENTEEN

"Keep your hands where we can see them, bitch." Two strange gunmen stood in the doorway holding an unconscious Franco between them. One waved his gun at her. She put her hands up. The men dropped Franco's limp, lifeless body onto the floor and slammed the door shut.

"What have you done to him?" She fought to keep her voice steady. "Where's Harris?"

"Lover boy will be okay, so long as you give us what we want. The other guy's swimming with the fishes."

Harris dead? She forced away the terror that pressed against her chest. *Focus, Jo, focus*. "Who are you?"

"We're your worst nightmare. Be a good girl and cooperate if you and lover boy want to live."

"Cooperate how?" Jo started to back up slowly. If she could push the hall table between her and them, she might have a chance to get her weapon. But there were two of them and one of her.

"Stop right there," said the second man, who'd been silent until now. He pointed his gun at her chest. "No funny stuff. You try any of that martial arts shit, and you're dead."

He glanced at his companion. "Frisk her."

The other man grabbed her shoulder and spun her around. She grunted as her forehead banged against the wall and he pulled her gun from her waistband.

"Nice piece." She heard her gun hit the floor, then the sound of him kicking it aside. Anger built in Jo, a gathering firestorm, but she fought back her rage. *Not now.*

Rough hands grasped Jo's shoulders, turned her, and slammed her against the wall again. She found herself face-to-face with the leader, their bodies inches apart. His flat, black eyes stared into hers. Expressionless, dead, they made Jo shiver. She almost gagged at the smell of stale whiskey on his breath.

"Give us the money," he said, "or you and your boy-friend are dead."

Jo gritted her teeth and resisted the urge to spit in his face. "I don't know what you're talking about."

"You know plenty. You live here. Where's the money?"

"*What* money?"

The thug pressed his hand against her throat. "Don't play dumb, bitch."

She struggled to breathe and gasped for air when he released his hold on her throat.

"We're not leaving until you tell us where the money is." He grabbed her arm and threw her toward the living room. "Time to talk."

She glanced back at Franco and saw him stir. Thank God. And what about Harris? She prayed he was alive. If anyone could survive, it was Harris. Hopefully, his SEAL training would kick in, wherever they'd taken him.

Dead Eyes gave her another shove. She faked a trip and reached out a hand to balance herself. He gripped her upper arm and squeezed hard, holding her upright. The other guy brought a chair from the dining room and set it in the center of the living room. He pulled out a piece of rope from the pocket of his jeans. These guys had come prepared.

178

"Sit." Dead Eyes pushed her into the chair. The other guy grabbed her arms and put them behind the high chair back, then proceeded to tie her hands at the wrists. Jo held her wrists slightly apart, but not so much that the thug would notice. Maybe they'd leave her legs free. She breathed a little easier when the man who'd tied her moved to stand before her, not holding another piece of rope. Big mistake.

She studied the men, imprinting their images onto her mind. Dead Eyes was short, but powerfully built, with thinning dark hair. The other man was taller, slimmer, with thick gray hair and a goatee. His watery blue eyes held no expression, as if his soul was long dead. She'd call him Cry Baby.

Dead Eyes moved closer, a hulking menacing figure that reminded her of a fiend in a horror movie. "Tell us where the money is."

"I told you, I don't know what you're talking about. What money?"

He slapped her across the face. Her head whipped around and her ears rang from the impact. His blow hit her with more force than DiGiacomo's had. She fought the wave of nausea that rose in her chest.

"You know Callahan's business," he said. "Give us the fucking money."

She'd gladly give them the money if she thought they'd go away and leave Franco and her alive. But she knew better. She had to keep them talking, had to stall for time. Maybe one of the neighbors had seen the guys pull Franco up the steps and called the police. Maybe Harris had gotten free and was on his way with the cops.

"Tell me what money you want. Maybe if I knew, I could help." She kept her voice calm and low.

The men looked at each other. Cry Baby turned his attention to her and grinned, exposing a gold front tooth. "You know what we're talkin' about. MacIntyre said he hid it here. Callahan knows. So do you." He leaned in close. "You're his woman, ain't you?"

She took shallow breaths, fought the urge to retch. "Franco doesn't tell me anything. I don't know anyone named MacIntyre."

"Lying bitch!" Dead Eyes hit her across the face again. The blow forced her to bite the inside of her cheek. She tasted blood. He stepped closer and squeezed her chin between his fingers. Tears flooded her eyes. "Look, bitch, MacIntyre said Callahan had the money. Talk, and we let you both live."

Time to change tactics. Most criminals were narcissistic and liked to have their egos stroked. "You didn't let Harris live. Did you know he's an ex-SEAL? Pretty hard to get past one of those guys. How'd you do it?"

"You ask too many fucking questions," Dead Eyes said.

But Cry Baby stepped forward and puffed out his chest. Bingo. "We greased the palms of the garage attendants."

Dead Eyes backhanded his accomplice in the arm. "What the fuck did you tell her that for?"

"She needs to know we mean business," Cry Baby said, rubbing his arm.

While their attention was diverted, Jo worked at the rope binding her and stole a glance at Franco. He lay where they'd left him, but his eyes were open and he stared directly at her. An understanding of what they needed to do passed between them and Jo blinked her eyes in acknowledgement.

The men turned back to her and she forced a smile. "You're smart guys. How do you know this MacIntyre?"

"Never met him," Dead Eyes said. "Sal heard about the money when he was locked up." He squeezed her chin again, forcing her to look into his eyes. "Now where's the money?"

"Sal?" The word reverberated through her brain.

"Our boss," Cry Baby said.

"You mean Sal DiGiacomo? He's your boss?"

"You deaf?" Dead Eyes growled. "Lucky for Sal they put the dude who stuck MacIntyre in the hole next to him. MacIntyre had a big mouth, and me and the boss owe some very bad people. They're getting a little anxious for their money. Sal figured he'd get his revenge on Callahan for fucking his wife and we'd get the money."

Jo blinked, processing the information. "The police have DiGiacomo. He's already looking at more jail time."

Dead Eyes shrugged. "It happens. We get the money, I pay off the debt, we split what's left. Sal gets out of the joint and he's got a nice investment waiting. He'll be out soon, like last time. He's got connections."

Jo angled her chin at Cry Baby. "What's in it for you?"

His gold front tooth glinted in the weak sunlight coming through the window. "Booze and broads. What else?"

What else indeed. "You can walk away now," she said to Cry Baby. "Walk now and I won't tell the police you're involved."

"Bitch!" Dead Eyes balled his hand into a fist and pulled his arm back, ready to swing at her, but Cry Baby grabbed his arm, stopping him.

"Knock her out and she can't talk. We got to get that money and get the fuck out of here."

Jo moved her wrists slowly, carefully so they wouldn't notice. A little bit more and she could slip her hands free.

"Go get Callahan," Dead Eyes rasped.

Panic clogged Jo's throat. She swallowed and took calming breaths while her mind assessed options.

Cry Baby swaggered toward Franco. He was a foot away from Franco's inert body when Franco rolled over, jumped up and head-butted the guy in the stomach, sending them both sprawling.

Jo's hands weren't freed yet, but she had no time. She stood, still tied to the chair, and rushed Dead Eyes with a head shot to his gut. He grunted and staggered backward. Working feverishly, she freed her hands and threw off the chair.

Grunts and the thud of blows filled the room as Franco and Cry Baby grappled on the floor.

Dead Eyes had regained his balance and pointed his gun at Jo. "Stay right there, bitch. Call Callahan off or he gets a bullet."

"You won't kill either of us. You need that money too bad."

"Try me."

"I will." She kicked the gun from his hand before he could get off a shot. She almost smiled at the shocked look on his face as the gun flew across the room. He made a dive for it and Jo dove after him, knocking him sideways and kicking the gun out of his reach. Holding onto her, he twisted and flipped her over. Her head hit the floor, but the Oriental rug cushioned the blow. He crouched over her and she kneed him in the groin. He yelped and bucked, holding his crotch. She rolled away and jumped up. The gun! Where the hell was it?

"Bitch! You'll pay for that!"

"Come and get me." Fighting for breath, she danced around the stumbling Dead Eyes, kicking him in the ribs, then dancing away before he could grab her. She needed time to get her weapon. When she kicked him in the groin again, he doubled over.

She spotted Dead Eye's gun just before she noticed Franco and Cry Baby caught in a macabre embrace, fighting over Cry Baby's weapon. Her heart lurched, but she couldn't help Franco, not until she dispatched Dead Eyes.

Head down, Dead Eyes charged her. She jumped as high as she could and landed a kick to his throat. He squealed and grabbed his neck, stumbling backward.

A gun went off. Jo's pulse spiked. She glanced at Franco. He'd wrestled the gun from Cry Baby. The thug sprang at Franco and the gun flew out of Franco's hand.

Dead Eyes charged her again. She went with the motion, using his own momentum against him. Neatly, she sidestepped him and gave him a shove into the nearest wall. He bounced off it like a rubber ball and struggled to stay upright as she grabbed the chair and swung it against his midsection. He roared but refused to go down. Her fist connected to his face, his neck, his chest, over and over until her knuckles were bloody. But like a wounded bull, he just kept coming. She feinted to the left.

"Give up, you sonofabitch," she snarled.

"Fuck you!" He shook his head and took a swing at her face. She feinted to the right.

Dead Eye's gun lay a few feet away. Jo dove for the weapon. She heard Dead Eye's footsteps close behind. He reached for her waistband as she grabbed the gun, jerked free and straightened.

Holding the gun, she pivoted to face him. He pounced. She fired. She fired again.

Screaming and holding his kneecaps, he sank to the floor.

Jo ran to Franco. He had the other guy down and was

sitting on top of him, his hands around the man's throat. Cry Baby struggled for air, trying to wrench away from Franco.

"I got this," Jo said, pointing the gun at Cry Baby. "It's okay, Franco. Let him go."

Franco released his hold and jumped off. "Get up real slow," she said to Cry Baby. "No funny moves or you're dead."

She jerked her head toward Franco. "My gun is in the hall. Get it and watch the other guy."

He raced to her gun, grabbed it and ran back into the living room. Dead Eyes was still screaming and swearing, clutching his knees. Franco aimed the gun at him. "Give me one good reason to shoot you again. Just one."

Jo blinked and Dead Eyes quit swearing. There was no mistaking that Franco meant it.

She nodded toward the nearest phone. "I need to call the—"

The front door crashed open, cutting her short. Uni-formed cops, guns drawn, raced into the room. Detective Morelli and Harris followed close behind.

CHAPTER EIGHTEEN

"Darlin', I'm sorry," Harris said for the umpteenth time as he, Jo and Franco trudged into Franco's house. It was past midnight now. They'd spent hours at the hospital having their wounds tended and giving statements to the police. Harris followed Jo into the living room while Franco closed what was left of the door. Jo saw Harris's jaw tighten as he paused, staring at the splintered molding surrounding the doorway. The police had finished processing the crime scene, but with the door broken, uniformed cops patrolled outside.

Jo strode to the middle of the living room, then turned to face Harris. "Quit beating yourself up. It's not your fault. This was planned and they were desperate. There were four of them and two of you."

"I let my guard down. I know better than that. And I let you down. You and Franco could have been killed."

"Hey, man," Franco said, coming into the room. "Jo's right. And if it weren't for you and Jo, I'd be dead." His expression sobered. "You saved my life. Harris, you almost got yourself killed too—knocked out, stuffed in a trunk, driven to the river. You've been through a lot. We all have."

Jo released a breath. "It's over. And we're all still standing." She looked at the broken door. "Can't say the same for your door. That thing's been through a lot. You need a new one."

Franco nodded. "I'll get a couple of my guys to put in a new door before daylight." He grinned. "I'll have them put the old back door in too and get rid of that ugly steel one."

He held out his arms to her. "Come here."

She went willingly into his embrace, needing his closeness and comfort. He held her against him and rubbed his hand up and down her back. "Thanks to you, we recovered the money too," Franco said. On their way to the hospital, Jo had told him about the money and repeated the information to the police.

Keeping an arm around Franco's waist, she turned to Harris. "I can picture the looks on those guys' faces when they opened the trunk of their car and you jumped out. At least Dead Eyes and Cry Baby will join DiGiacomo in jail along with the thugs they hired to kill you."

"Can't keep an old SEAL like me down."

"When those men said you were swimming with the fishes, my heart nearly stopped."

"I didn't feel so good about it myself. I wasn't in the mood for swimming. When do you leave for Tucson?"

She jerked her head up at his sudden change of topic. "I'm not sure," she said, deliberately focusing on Harris.

He smiled. "Well, it's been good working with you, as always, darlin'. But now I need to get home." Digging a wrapped piece of hard candy from his pocket, he headed to the door. He unwrapped the candy and slid it into his mouth.

Smiling, Jo and Franco followed.

"Thanks for everything, man." Franco held out his hand to shake Harris's. "I owe you. If you ever need anything, I'm here."

"Been a pleasure knowing you, Franco. You're a good

man." Harris turned to Jo and held out his arms.

She stepped into them and hugged him tight. "See you soon."

He hugged her, then held her at arm's length. "Maybe not. You've got a new teammate." With a smile, he nodded at Franco. "Take good care of her."

"I will," Franco said.

Jo frowned. What did Franco mean by that? She'd be in Tucson while he'd be in Philadelphia. She'd take care of herself—like always.

They said their goodbyes to Harris and walked back to the living room.

"How about a drink?" Franco asked. "Some wine?"

Jo sank onto the sectional and shrugged. "Why not? I'm not on duty anymore. And I'm too wound up to sleep." She glanced at the Oriental rug. "We need to clean the blood off the rug. Dead Eyes made a huge mess."

"I'll send it out later to get cleaned. I'm not worried about it. I can always get a new one. We're okay and that's all that matters."

Favoring her sore knuckles, she gingerly took the glass of burgundy wine Franco offered. "I have to write my report to Logan."

Franco sat beside her. "You called Logan from the hospital. The report can wait. You need to rest. We both do. Unfortunately, I need to go to work tomorrow. I have a meeting I can't put off, but I'll go in late."

She sipped her wine, enjoying the slide of the rich liquid down her throat. More of her tension dissolved with each sip of her drink.

Franco cradled his wine glass between his hands, his profile to her. "You were right all along. It had to do with

Mac." He shook his head. "I think on some level, I knew the money the thugs wanted involved Mac. I was in denial. Who would have thought Mac hid it here? No wonder he was so smug when the authorities arrested him."

Jo set her glass on the table and touched Franco's chin, drawing his attention. "You can't blame yourself for what Mac did. Did he have a key?"

"Of course. He was my best friend. He'd stay in the guest room sometimes when he'd had too much to drink." Franco took a long sip of wine, then set his glass next to hers. "I guess he figured it was safe here. At least I can give the money back to the kids." He shook his head. "Mac didn't figure on getting killed."

"But he did figure on coming back for the money. He told the wrong people about it before he died."

"And here I was, a sitting duck. Tell me something, Jo."

"What?" The intense look in Franco's eyes made her shift uncomfortably.

"When you found that money, didn't you, even for a little while, think I had something to do with the theft? That I was in cahoots with Mac?"

She slid her gaze from his.

"Jo?"

"It crossed my mind for about a second," she said, turning back to him. "But the Franco Callahan I've come to know couldn't be that devious, and he wouldn't lie to me. I just had to figure out how the money was planted without you suspecting anything."

Relief washed over his face and his eyes softened. "Thank you for that. I'm not sure anyone else would have had such faith in me." He took both her hands in his and kissed her sore knuckles. "My poor Jo. Hurt because of me."

"Occupational hazard." She leaned forward and planted a gentle kiss on his lips. "You've got to be careful for the next few days. Getting hit with the butt of a gun isn't good for your head."

"I have a hard head. I'll be fine." He blew out a breath. "It's been a long day. Let's get to bed."

Sunlight teased Jo's eyes open. The brightness in the room told her the sun had fully risen. Once again she'd slept in Franco's arms. He lay on his side next to her this morning, one arm across her waist, keeping her close. When they'd gone to bed, both of them were too exhausted to do anything more than snuggle together. She would like to sleep in his arms every night. But she wouldn't be another of his women, one of his toys.

She rolled over, shifting away from him, and winced. Her whole body ached from her fight with Dead Eyes. She'd have some major bruises. She slid her arms from under the comforter and held up her battered hands. Her knuckles would heal quickly. They always did.

"Morning," Franco said. He took her in his arms and kissed her. "How do you feel?"

"Sore as hell. How about you?"

He grimaced. "The same. We're a pair, aren't we?"

They'd make a good pair in life too. She bit back the words.

"I want you," he whispered. "But I don't want to hurt you."

She grazed a finger over his bottom lip. "I won't break."

He threw back the covers, then rolled her onto her back. His eyes, blue flames, trailed over her naked body, heating

CARA MARSI

her to her core. "You are an amazing and beautiful woman."

"Make love to me."

"With pleasure."

He kissed her tenderly, carefully, then kissed his way down her body with exquisite slowness until she writhed under him. When he kissed the inside of her thighs and parted her folds to slide his finger into her, she moaned softly. "You are so ready for me," he said, awe in his voice.

His mouth replaced his finger. She twisted her head on the pillow and curled her fingers around the sheet, moaning when he found her bud. Licks of fire spread through her body until she was hot, restless, wild. Her breasts were tight and aching for Franco's touch. Like a volcano, her powerful climax erupted in molten waves. Finally, she lay spent beneath him.

His breathing rough, he slipped away and opened his night table drawer. When he'd pulled on protection, he positioned himself above her.

"No," she said. "I want to make love to you."

Smiling, he rolled over and took her with him, pulling her on top of him. She straddled him and ran her fingers down his hardness. "You're exquisite," she breathed.

"I can't wait much longer," he said. "You feel so good." He brushed hair back from her face. "Jo, I …"

She lifted herself to accommodate his length and took him fully into her. Groaning, he spanned her waist with his hands and lifted her gently over his fullness, in and out. She wondered what he'd begun to say, but the thought fled at the feel of him sliding in and out of her willing body. A fierce, desperate need filled her as he slid his hands up to cup her breasts. She wanted to please him, to give him some measure of what he'd given her. She threw back her head and moved over him, faster and faster. Her hair brushed past her shoulders, the movement soft and sensual. Franco's low groans spurred her on. That she could satisfy this strong, masculine man made her heart ready to burst with pride and feminine power. She gloried in his strength and in the love she felt for him. She cried out his name as her climax hit her hard and fast. He shuddered with his own climax. They were one, and she was complete at last.

Afterward, they lay in each other's arms, satiated and spent.

Franco drew her closer and kissed her temple. "I told you when this was over, I'd take you somewhere exotic and isolated. I want you all to myself. I want to make love to you all day."

"Sounds heavenly," she said, scrunching closer to him. "But I have a job to get back to."

He pulled away to look into her eyes. "I'm sure Logan will give you some time off. A friend of mine owns a place in the Caymans. I know he'll let us use it. I'll call him today."

"Then after that, what happens to us, Franco?" She was afraid of the answer but she had to ask.

His expression sobered. "I can't promise anything, Jo," he said quietly, maybe even regretfully. "I'm not the settling down type. Stay with me here for awhile. We'll have fun. Be together."

Her heart shattered into a million pieces, like crystal hit by a hammer. She really was just another woman to him.

Fighting tears, she scooted to the other side of the bed. "Sorry, Franco. Doesn't work for me. I'm going back to Tucson. Today." She slid out of bed and strode toward the door.

"Don't leave, Jo. Not yet. Stay with me."

She turned to face him in all his naked glory, confusion

on his beautiful face. She loved him so much. She doubted she'd love anyone like this again. Her heart broke a little more.

"What do you want from me, Jo?"

"Something you apparently can't give. Go to work, Franco. I'll be gone by the time you get home."

He stepped back as if stung, but before she had time to regret her words, he smiled that insolent player smile she knew all too well. "I see. Well then take the company jet," he offered almost casually. "You deserve that at least. I'll have Ruth make the arrangements. She'll call you later."

Jo stood in the entry hall, her duffel bag at her feet. While they'd slept, two of Franco's site foremen had replaced the broken front door with a sturdy new one and switched out the steel back door to the original one. Everything in Franco's life was settling back into place. Her life would never be quite the same again.

She pulled the collar of the leather jacket a little closer over her silk blouse and adjusted her skinny jeans. She'd left most of the beautiful clothes Franco had bought her. She'd taken some of the delicate lingerie, a few pairs of jeans, some tops, the large designer handbag, and the leather jacket with the matching boots that she wore now. And the silver stiletto sandals.

She'd changed in the time she'd been there. Franco had taught her to appreciate her femininity, to be proud of her looks. Taught her that no matter how she dressed, she was the same person inside. She hadn't lost herself as she'd once feared. More importantly, he'd helped her on a deeper level. Because of him, she'd let go of her demons, seen them diminish on her soul's horizon until they were gone, where they wouldn't bother her ever again. He'd freed her sensuality, made her a complete woman. She'd always be grateful. She blinked back tears. So why wasn't she happy?

Franco's assistant had made all the arrangements for the Callahan jet to fly her to Tucson, had even hired a car to drive her to the airport. Her ride would be here any minute.

Part of her wanted to cry, but another part of her was dead. Franco didn't love her. She refused to be one of his kept women, someone he'd discard when he tired of her, the way he had Lynn and the others. She deserved better than that.

A black limo glided to a stop outside. Her ride was here.

He was an idiot. Franco looked out the large window in his office and stared across the city to the statue of William Penn atop Philadelphia's City Hall. "I'll bet you were never this stupid, were you, old Billy?"

Raking fingers through his hair, he paced his office. Jo was gone. And he had let her walk away. What kind of fool was he? He'd been living under his player image for too long. He'd gotten used to hiding his true self from the world. Despite what he'd been through the past four years—the fear that others would see the real him and find him wanting had stayed with him. Jo had seen through him. He didn't have to hide anymore. She'd shown him that.

And he'd let her go.

He strode out of his office to his assistant's desk. "Ruth, did our jet leave for Tucson yet?"

She glanced at the clock. "It should have taken off about fifteen minutes ago."

He swore. "Then move heaven and earth to get me on

193

a flight west. Today. Any flight to Arizona. Charter a plane if you have to."

"I'll do my best."

Half an hour later Franco stared at his computer screen, not seeing the figures before him. He pushed away the pile on his desk, scattering the papers. Shoving a hand through his hair, he dropped his head into his hands. He'd lost Jo. She'd never forgive him for being such a jackass.

"Heard you need a bodyguard, Callahan."

The sultry female voice jerked Franco's attention. He lifted his head. His heart started to pound. He swallowed hard, not quite believing what he saw. He made a last grab at his careless cool. "Well, if it isn't Josephine Fortune. What are you doing here?"

She stepped into the room and deposited her duffel bag on the floor. "I'm here to save your sorry ass."

He got up from his desk and marched toward the door. Leaning out, he said, "Take the rest of the day off, Ruth. I won't need that flight to Tucson after all."

She smiled. "Anything you say."

Franco closed his office door and turned to Jo. His gaze scanned her. Dressed in a leather jacket, pale green silk blouse, jeans that hugged her lithe body, and wearing high-fashion boots, she was hip, cool, and sexy. A far cry from the fatigue-clad spitfire who'd first shown up at his door. But inside she was the same Jo, the warm, wonderful woman he loved.

"What are you going to save me from?" he asked.

She moved closer and ran her hand down his necktie. "Tucson?"

"I was coming to get you." He grabbed her hand and pressed it to his chest. "What do I need saving from?"

"Yourself."

His heart still pounding, he smiled. "Why?"

"Because without me, you'll end up a bitter, lonely old man. I couldn't let that happen."

Her full lips, pink and soft, beckoned. He bent and took her mouth in a tender kiss, letting her know with his body how much she meant to him. Pulling away, he slid his palm down her arm. "I agree I need saving."

"What kind of reward do I get for saving you?"

He laughed. "Demanding, aren't you?"

"You ain't seen nothing yet, Callahan."

He looked deeply into her eyes. "Don't ever leave me again."

"Don't ever send me away again."

He slid his finger across her lips. "I love you, Jo Fortune. I've loved you for a very long time."

She wrapped her arms around his neck. "Even when I wore fatigues and combat boots?"

"I love you for who you are, not for what you wear."

"You could have told me sooner, you know."

"Not really. I'd held onto my player image so long I thought I was beyond redemption. My feelings for you scare me. Always have."

She stood on tiptoe and kissed him. "My feelings for you scare me too."

He crushed her to him and buried his face in her hair. "Jo. My Jo. I almost lost you."

"You couldn't lose me if you tried, Callahan. You taught me to have faith in myself, to believe in myself. I knew deep down you loved me." She pulled away and smiled up at him. "You were too dense to know it. I'm no quitter. I wasn't about to give up on you." She frowned. "You need to do one thing for me."

"Anything, sweetheart."

"You need to tell your family about your community center, the charity, everything you've done for those kids, the truth about Mac. Come clean. Don't hide who you are anymore. You'll never be happy hiding parts of yourself."

He took a step back. "It won't be easy. I've kept that part of myself locked away for so long."

"Do it for me."

"I'd give you the world if I could, Jo."

"I don't want the world. I want you, the real you, the honest, big-hearted guy I love."

The love shining from her magnificent green eyes was almost his undoing. He swallowed the lump in his throat and took her hand. "You're the only person to really have faith in me, to believe in me. For you, I'll tell my family everything."

Still holding her hand, he sank to the floor on one knee.

"What are you doing?" she asked, startled.

"You're more precious to me than gold, Jo Fortune. Will you marry me?"

Tears sparkled from her eyes. He'd never seen her look more beautiful and he'd never loved her more.

"Of course I'll marry you, you big lug. Someone has to look after you."

With a laugh, he straightened and grabbed her by the waist. He swung her around until they were both breathless from laughing. He set her down and gazed into her eyes. "We'll get married as soon as we can. We'll go shopping for rings tonight."

She wound her arms around his neck. "I love you, Franco Callahan." She stroked his face. "I have for a very long time."

"And I love you."

EPILOGUE

"I'm so nervous." Jo stood in front of the mirror in the dressing room off the church vestibule and stared at her reflection, not quite believing the stylish woman staring back was really her. The strapless white gown with ruching on the sweetheart neckline and delicate lace over satin skimmed her body to end in a small train. A green satin ribbon adorned with a crystal brooch wound around her waist and trailed down her back.

Her hair, thanks to Anita, fell in soft waves to her shoulders and shone with gold highlights. She hadn't wanted a veil. Instead, a garland of white rosebuds circled her head. Her makeup, also thanks to Anita, was perfect. But Jo knew the sparkle in her eyes wasn't from makeup but from her happiness. The June day was brilliant. She'd soon marry the man she adored. Tomorrow they'd leave for the Cayman Islands to spend a week alone in Franco's friend's house, isolated from the rest of the world. A week to make love, to laugh, to start their life together.

Next to her, Doriana gave Jo an assessing look. "You're gorgeous."

"You are," Anita echoed.

Jo blinked back tears. "I still can't believe today's my wedding day."

"You'd better not cry," Anita said. "You'll screw up the

terrific makeup job I did."

Doriana and Jo laughed.

"That's better," Doriana said. "A bride should laugh on her wedding day."

Anita put her hand on her hip. "Fine advice from you. You cried buckets the day you married Logan."

Doriana patted her protruding belly. "I did, didn't I?"

Jo's heart swelled as she looked from Doriana to Anita. Her new family. She had a family now, one who loved and accepted her. And a man who showed her every day how much he worshipped her. He listened to her, respected her opinions, believed in her. In everything he did and everything he said, he made her feel cherished and real and loved. Overwhelmed with happiness, she smiled at her two bridesmaids.

Doriana, at seven-months pregnant, had never looked more beautiful. Both women looked amazing in the pale green silk dresses that complemented their raven hair and creamy skin.

"You're next, Anita," Jo said.

Anita shook her head. "Not me. I'm perfectly happy on my own."

Doriana raised an eyebrow. "I doubt that."

Jo grinned at their good-natured teasing. Taking a deep breath, she scanned the small room in the historic Philadelphia church. The scent of roses wafted through the open stained-glass windows, their sweetness holding the promise of sunny days and moonlit nights in the arms of the man she loved. Their reception after the ceremony would be held on the extensive grounds of an elegant mansion on Philadelphia's Main Line. A friend of Dan Callahan's owned the house and gladly lent it to them for the wedding festivities.

A knock at the door made them turn. Lena, beautiful in beige silk, peeked in. "We're almost ready."

"Oh, God." Jo pressed a hand to her stomach where the resident butterflies were going crazy.

"Jo, things will be fine," Lena said, stepping into the room. A smile on her face, she approached Jo. "You look beautiful. My son is a lucky man. We're lucky to have you in our family."

Jo blinked tears away and swallowed. "Thanks, Lena."

"Call me mom if you're comfortable."

"Mom." Tears slipped down Jo's cheeks.

Lena hugged her, then swiped at her own tears. "Thank you for helping my son. We're so proud of all he's done. We don't understand why he couldn't tell us before."

"It's complicated. Tell him how proud you are of him. Franco needs to know that."

"We've told him," Lena said. "And we'll continue to tell him."

The strains of Pachelbel's *Canon in D* from the string quartet in the church filled the room. Doriana and Anita's cue.

"Oh, God," Jo said again.

Lena gave Jo another hug. "I've got to get out there. The usher's waiting to escort me down the aisle."

"Go, Mom," Doriana said. "We can't go until you're seated."

Lena hurried from the room.

"Don't worry, Jo. Everything will be fine," Doriana said, giving her a hug.

"My turn," Anita said. She hugged Jo. "Go get that cousin of mine."

Feeling slightly more relaxed, Jo grabbed her bouquet

of white rosebuds and followed her bridesmaids from the room. Logan, handsome as always in a dark blue suit with a white rosebud boutonniere, stepped from the shadows. His hazel eyes, flecked with gold, shone with love when he looked at Doriana. He bent to give his wife a peck on the cheek.

"You're beautiful, Dorie," he said.

She patted her stomach. "I'm fat."

He laughed. "You're always beautiful to me."

Logan turned to Jo and held out his arm. Holding her bouquet in front of her, she tucked her free arm into his. He leaned down and kissed her on the cheek. "You're beautiful too, little one."

"Don't call me that." Despite her words, she couldn't stop the laugh that bubbled up. He'd given her the nickname in the Army and used it whenever he wanted to tease her.

"Franco's a lucky man," he said.

"I know he is."

Logan laughed as he and Jo lined up behind Anita and Doriana where they waited at the church doorway for their cues.

When the bridesmaids were halfway down the white carpet, the strains of *Here Comes the Bride* replaced *Canon in D*. It was Jo's turn. The butterflies in her stomach stirred again, but she ignored them. Her arm in Logan's she felt as if she floated down the carpet toward the altar where the priest waited. The guests watching with smiles on their faces passed by in a blur. She recognized Judge Benjamin and his wife Charlene, the couple who'd helped her when she was seventeen. When she walked past Harris, he smiled and gave her a thumbs-up sign.

Then all else faded when Jo spotted Franco. In

his dark blue suit with his hair swept back, he could have jumped from the pages of a fashion magazine. But his vibrancy, his lust for life, and the love shining from his blue eyes couldn't be found in any magazine. Joy blossomed in her heart and she smiled. He returned her smile, and her heart pounded. Only Franco and she existed alone in their private loving world.

When they reached the altar, Logan placed her hand in Franco's and gave her another kiss on the cheek. "Be happy, little one," he said before taking his place in the front row next to Franco's parents.

Franco's blue eyes darkened as he took Jo's hand. "I love you," he whispered into her ear. "You're the most beautiful and amazing woman I've ever known. My Jo. My love. My future and my fortune."

* Thank you for reading *Franco's Fortune*. Please turn the page if you'd like to read an excerpt from *Luke's Temptation* (Redemption Book 3) *

***

LUKE'S TEMPTATION

by

Cara Marsi

CHAPTER ONE

Anita Santisi locked her car with her remote and juggled her packages as she strode toward her condo loft in an upscale suburb of Philadelphia. With the street lights illuminating her way in the darkness, she struggled to hold onto her packages and picked her way up the steep steps in her stiletto boots.

"Why the heck did I buy so many Christmas gifts?" she muttered. But she knew. She loved buying baby clothes and toys for her cousins' babies. And as honorary aunt, it was her duty to spoil them.

She got to her front door and let out a small cry. Her insides shook. The packages fell from her hands to land in a pile by her feet. Her front door hung open on its hinges with a huge hole at the bottom as if someone had kicked it in with heavy boots.

She did a quick scan of the area. No one else was around. Forcing air into lungs that felt ready to burst, she turned and ran down the steps, stumbling in her haste. Grabbing the handrail, she caught herself. On unsteady legs, she gripped the railing and hurried the rest of the way down. Near the bottom, she lost her balance and almost fell, but strong arms grabbed her and kept her upright.

"What's wrong?" a male voice asked.

She screamed and tore loose from the stranger. When she looked up into deep brown eyes, almost black in their intensity, her heart rate kicked up a notch. Had he been walking along the sidewalk, or did he follow her from her house?

Gulping breaths, she backed away. Her attention on the stranger, she pulled her phone out of her purse. With shaking fingers, she dialed 911. When the operator answered, Anita said, "My home's been broken into. The intruder might still be inside."

With a promise the police were on their way and an admonition from the operator not to go into her house, Anita disconnected. Still clutching her phone, she put more distance between her and the tall stranger.

"Your house was broken into?" he asked. "I'm sorry. I'll stay with you and wait for the police."

"They'll be here any minute. I'm fine now. You can leave." She licked her lips, and not taking her eyes off the stranger, she fished in her purse for her car's remote. It had a panic button. If he dared move toward her, she'd set it off.

He nodded toward the adjoining condos. "I don't see how I can leave since I live here."

She swallowed. "Live here?"

"I'm your new neighbor. I thought this was a safe neighborhood."

"Neighbor?" Trying to wrap her mind around that

surprising information, words failed her and she could only continue to stare up at him. Her loft, in a restored warehouse, was one of two condos that shared a common wall. Each had a private entrance, the doors a few feet from each other. The loft next to hers had stood empty the past year since the owner transferred to Japan for his work. She'd heard someone rented it recently.

Her alleged new neighbor furrowed his brow. "You okay?"

Fairly sure he wasn't her intruder or an ax murderer, Anita still had to be cautious. She put her finger over the panic button on her remote.

"I'm Luke Corrado." He held out his hand. "This is a hell of a way to meet."

"It sure is. I'm Anita Santisi." She decided caution trumped politeness and didn't take the proffered hand. Still on guard in case he made a movement toward her, she looked more closely at him. He was easy on the eyes, with his short black hair and those dark eyes that watched her as if he thought her the most fascinating woman he'd ever met. She'd noticed a dimple in his cheek when he smiled. Nice lips, not too thin, not too full, just right for kissing. Smooth olive skin stretched taut over high cheekbones, inviting her to touch.

"Like what you see?" he asked, showing that dimple again.

Heat suffused her face. He might be eye candy, but he was arrogant. Anita didn't tolerate arrogant men. And she still didn't trust him. She sent him a look she'd perfected, one that usually sent grown men scrambling for cover. Apparently, it wasn't sending this man anywhere. He looked contrite, or tried to look contrite.

"I'm sorry," he said. "That didn't come out right. I sounded like a jerk."

"Yeah, you did."

He gave her that dimpled smile that made warmth

swirl through her despite her anxiety and the late November chill.

His magnetism tempted her to scan the rest of him. His black leather jacket and black sweater didn't disguise the width of his shoulders or the breadth of his chest. Close-fitting jeans hugged long legs that seemed to go on forever. All in all, one hot package.

"Let's start over. I'm your new neighbor, Luke Corrado."

Before she could respond, lights flashed in the darkness as three police cars pulled up to the curb.

***

*I hope you enjoyed this excerpt of *Luke's Temptation* by Cara Marsi. If you'd like to read the book in its entirety, please check with your favorite online retailer for availability, or visit Cara's website at CaraMarsi.com for purchase info.*

BOOKS BY CARA MARSI

A Catered Romance
A Cat's Tale & Other Love Stories
(All stories in this anthology are available separately)
A Cinderella Christmas
A Groom for Christmas
Accidental Love
Cursed Mates
Her Forever Husband
Her Snow White Christmas (Snow Globe Magic Book 1)
Logan's Redemption (Redemption Book 1)
Franco's Fortune (Redemption Book 2)
Luke's Temptation (Redemption Book 3)
Love Potion
Loving Or Nothing
Murder, Mi Amore
Storm of Desire
Sweet Temptations
Sweet Temptations Boxed Set
The One Who Got Away
The Marriage Coin (Anthology)
The Ring
Wedding Dreams Boxed Set

Coming 2015, Capri Nights
Also Coming 2015, Her Frog Prince Holiday (Snow Globe
Magic Book 2)

Read excerpts at www.caramarsi.com
All books available at online booksellers
A Catered Romance, A Groom for Christmas, Franco's
Fortune, Logan's Redemption, Loving Or Nothing, Luke's
Temptation, and Murder, Mi Amore are also available in
print

An award-winning and eclectic author, Cara Marsi is published in romantic suspense, paranormal romance, and contemporary romance. She loves a good love story, and believes that everyone deserves a second chance at love. Sexy, sweet, thrilling, or magical, Cara's stories are first and foremost about the love. Treat yourself today, with a taste of romance.

When not traveling or dreaming of traveling, Cara and her husband live on the East Coast in a house ruled by two spoiled cats who compete for attention.

Find out more about Cara and her books and sign up for her newsletter at her website at CaraMarsi.com. She's on Twitter, Goodreads, Facebook, and Pinterest and is always interested in meeting new friends.

***

www.ingramcontent.com/pod-product-compliance
Lightning Source LLC
Chambersburg PA
CBHW061155170626
46809CB00003B/1110